BLESSINGS *on the* SHEEP DOG

BLESSINGS
on the
SHEEP DOG

Stories by

GERDA SAUNDERS

SOUTHERN METHODIST
UNIVERSITY PRESS
Dallas

Requests for permission to reproduce material from this work should be sent to:
  Rights and Permissions
  Southern Methodist University Press
  PO Box 750415
  Dallas, Texas 75275-0415

Cover art: *Kirsten and Pop.* Courtesy of Sean Graff, Salt Lake City, Utah.
Design by Tom Dawson Graphic Design

LIBRARY OF CONGRESS CATALOGING-IN-PUBLICATION DATA
Saunders, Gerda.
  Blessings on the Sheep Dog : stories / by Gerda Saunders.—1st ed.
    p. cm.
  ISBN 0-87074-468-2 (alk. paper)
    1. South African Americans—Fiction. 2. United States—Social life and customs—Fiction. 3. South Africa—Social life and customs—Fiction. I. Title.

PS3619.A825 B57 2002
813'.6—dc21

                                                                2002019373

Printed in the United States of America on acid-free paper
10   9   8   7   6   5   4   3   2   1

for Marissa and Newton,
whose fresh perspectives continue to thrill me

for Lynne, Shen, and Kirstin,
who read my writing with candor and embrace
me with blindness

and, of course, for Peter,
who can say my name

Contents

A Sudden New City

What Heila hears outside the tractor cab when she wakes up is not the coo of the farm's turtledoves, but the squabble of the town square's pigeons. The flock takes to the air with a silky rustle and forms a cloud above General Hertzog's head with the white undersides of their wings. Heila thinks of Miss Stein, disappointed in love, jumping from Majuba's Rock and drifting, borne by her petticoats, down to the swimming hole where seven naked native boys saved her. Miss Stein, dead now. And Heila, who then was wide-eyed about the power of love, old.

In the first light everything on the square looks a little bit different from what Heila imagined when they arrived in town under cover of the dark. Last night, when the Snyman boy called to say the farmers' protest was going ahead, Heila told him she and Jacobus would come in the morning because she did not see so well to drive at night anymore. But their neighbor would not hear of it. "Mandela is going to be out within the month," he said. "He's going to take away our farms and give them to the kaffirs. We've got to come out strong. Tonight."

Heila thought of their tractor's tall wheels, and how hard it was to get up into the cab and find all those switches in the dark, but she said yes, they would leave right away, and woke up Jacobus, who was asleep in front of the TV. Now she was glad the drive was behind her, their tractor safely parked, even though the only spot she could find when they at long last got there was at the far end of the square, the side that faces the horse's tail.

So many farmers came that their tractors and planters and tillers form a complete circle around the lawn surrounding the General's statue. A few smaller trucks are even squeezed in between those chained-down benches and the trees with the purple flowers. Heila sniffs the air, but all she gets inside the tractor cab is the paper smell of her own skin and the stink of Jacobus's flatulence. She finds the window catch and manages to move it an inch. Through the gap she can see more clearly: on the other side of the tree the Snyman boy's combine harvester shows red through the flowers, and she had thought of it as blue all night!

One of the protesters is walking by between their tractor and the General. Heila leans forward on the steering wheel to see who it is, but the man has his hat on and could be anyone. She keeps staring through the glass until it becomes a mirror in which she can see herself, and growing from her hip, Jacobus sleeping on the seat beside her. *Till death us do part*, she thinks.

Or maybe it won't be death.

This thing about the farm—now that a buyer has finally appeared, Jacobus won't sell.

Jacobus believes what the Snyman boy told him—the buyer is an agent of the government; the government wants to buy *their* farms to give to the blacks. Heila imagines Winnie Mandela at the kitchen sink instead of herself, soap bubbles edged with rainbows glinting on her hands. She laughs at the picture in her head. That's not how it would be—they probably won't even use the sink. Not used to anything, these blacks. In Rhodesia they moved into the white houses and did not even use the stove. Cooked on a fire in the living room, made with yellowwood torn from the lintels. Heila imagines flames curling around the embuia of her sideboard, sees heat popping out the beveled glass doors and cracking the mirrored shelves. She shakes her head and touches her cheek to the cool glass. That's not how it would be. She would take her sideboard with her, of course. She doesn't care what they do to the house. As long as *she* can get away from the farm with its work and its sullen blacks lurking everywhere. To a safe, tidy flat in the same retirement complex as Kay and May.

Heila watches her hands stroke the molded plastic of the steering wheel. Ouma Mave's hands come to her: rheumatic claws, one clamped around a crotchet hook, a web of raveling work swaying from the other. Offered as a gift when done. An out-of-round doily, a baby dress for a newborn monster. "It's the idea," Ma used to say.

Hands tied to life with work. Heila's own, fisting into the space between the skin and the carcass of the newborn lamb. Coming out smelling of the private smell of death. Swishing the pelt through the wash water, lifting it streaming onto the burlap-covered frame. Tugging and nudging, a paw to each corner. And later, peeling the cured skins from the burlap: the hairs, too short to curl, dried to watered-silk smoothness. Like the finger waves Karl Meyer used to press into his hair.

Karl Meyer came over from his father's watch shop to court Heila when she was twenty-two and an old maid. She had taken a job at Mukherjee's Coolie Shop and on her first day Karl walked over to see if the new *London Mix* was in. Heila lifted the bottles onto the counter: with sticky red balls that smelled like nasturtiums; with peppermint hearts that said "Kiss Me"; with shiny black licorice ropes, with Turkish delight, with jelly babies in rainbow colors. He took an hour to pick a handful of sweets, asking her opinion on the color and flavor of every single one. When he was done, she poured his selection into a pocket of butcher paper she had folded into a funnel and closed off at the bottom with a twist. As soon as he paid, he gave them to her! *The Germans marry Germans*, Kay and May warned, sitting around the Sunday table with their new husbands. But she was the older sister, she did not believe them. She said no to a second helping of canfruit and custard, her favorite, so she could go off to spread the plaid rug under the river sage for her and Karl.

But it is not Karl asleep beside her on the tractor's other seat. It is Jacobus. His mouth has fallen open. Spittle funneled along a fold in his cheek shivers on his earlobe with each breath. She feels a softening in her chest for a moment, a scribbling of warmth rising to her neck. Jacobus had been good to her. When Frederik was born he branded two ewe-lambs for her, and another two at Hennie's birth. Through the years she had built up her own flock. Heila feels for her handbag on the floor between her feet. The money for her pelts she had put in a savings book. A lot of money by now. Enough for a flat, she thinks, like Kay and May's. Or a smaller one, for one person, if Jacobus refuses to leave. As long as there is room for her sideboard, her inheritance from Ouma Mave. With its rattling mirror shelves. With its conversation pieces. *A pair of miniature shoes.* Ouma Mave's breath on the glass as she told: of her brother, Uncle Gervase, a strapping man when they took him off to the concentration camp, an eighty-pound skeleton when they released him. With nothing. No coat, no pocket watch, no sense. His shirt wrapped about the miniature high-heeled pumps he'd molded from chewed bread crusts for his betrothed. *A cube of wedding cake.* The catch in Ouma Mave's voice as she remembered: Aunt Suster, stricken on the eve of her wedding with a fast-killing grippe. Buried in her wedding gown, the wedding cake cut up and handed around as a remembrance at the funeral. *Taste. It's still sweet.* The grey icing flower trembling on Ouma Mave's palm. Kay and May, and Maria, refusing with a shudder. Not Heila—she tasted.

Heila opens the cab door softly not to wake Jacobus, and feels for the step with her foot. From ground level the laager of farm machines around the square makes the skyline of a sudden new city. Heila asks the way to the toilets from a nice young man sitting with his mug of coffee on the General's pedestal. What's going to happen to these nice young men now they're going to let Mandela out? It's just as well that not one of their boys had shown an interest in the farm. Such a disappointment to Jacobus. Their boys had seen this thing coming, always arguing with their father. They had set themselves up for the new South Africa, each in his own way. Frederik with his franchise, all those soft chairs and couches, and scatter cushions the exact shade of the lamps. He even has an ad on TV. His hand pointing straight at her: *Now YOU have an uncle in the furniture business.* And Hennie, like Uncle Gervase, always against the stream. It broke Oupa Piet's heart when Gervase, his own son, refused to join the Rebellion in '14. *This thing in our nation has set brother against brother, father against son.* Her Hennie, doctoring blacks when he could have any job he wanted at the nice new hospital. "Tell your son he can come work here anytime," Dr. Taylor told her when she went in for the dizziness.

More people are awake when Heila returns. At their tractor the Snyman boy's wife hands her a mug of coffee. Heila remembers her name. Susie. Such a nice woman.

"Did you and the uncle manage to get some sleep?" Susie asks.

"At our age you don't need much," Heila jokes.

Jacobus awake at three or four every morning. Wiggling about in bed till five, then bumping and clattering fit to wake the dead. Out the door with his lunchbox tucked under his arm by five thirty. When Frederik slept over for her birthday, he couldn't believe it. "Why don't you get someone to do it, Pa?" he asked. "You can afford it." Heila kept quiet in front of Frederik, but she knew that was not true: Jacobus cannot afford help, because he had to buy a fancy new tractor that he cannot even drive. When all he plants these days are a few rows of vegetables. "Here, some tomatoes for you, Frederik." The way his top lip quivers when he says that. Jacobus, so important when the children visit. To show he can still do things.

Jacobus comes down from the cab clutching the loaf of bread *she* stayed up to bake while he slept in front of the TV. He stands across from her for a moment with his legs a step too wide apart, picking off flakes of charcoaled crust. Accusing her. Yeast bubbles. From not kneading properly. Grey lumpiness tied together with holes. Her head feels like that nowadays. One of the things she used to know was how to make finger paint out of flour and water. With drops of green and red and yellow food coloring. For Hennie and Frederik and little Maidie. She forgot to bring a bread knife or butter or jam. What could she have been thinking of?

Jacobus takes the loaf over to a folding table that the Snymans are setting up. He is showing off with it. "Fresh-baked last night before we left. I won't touch shop bread." He pulls that face. "Never have. Where's the butter, Heila?"

Heila pretends not to hear. Who is he to prove she's not the same? He's old too. He failed the eye test for his driver's license. The Snyman boy drags over a folding chair for her. Then he eats three slices of her bread, plain. "It's too good to ruin with butter or jam," he says.

"Thank you," Heila says. She feels her mouth go prim with

the pleasure of the compliment. She wants to sit in this chair and feel this good for the rest of the day. She feels for her handbag slung across the armrest of the chair. A hiccup of excitement rises in her throat. Jacobus said they would have time for tea with Kay and May when this is over. The last time they visited Kay and May, a sign was up: "Flats for sale." She's been thinking. While Kay and May listen to Jacobus's stories, she would go over to talk to the manager. She would show him her savings book, enough money for a flat. Women could buy flats now. Kay and May did.

Shouts are coming from behind the Snyman boy's harvester. The Snyman boy walks over and climbs up onto one of the big wheels. He talks to someone on the other side and then turns around to tell the people gathering in the square what is going on. "There is a bunch of blacks here," he says. "They say they're coming from the station and they want to go to work. They want us to move so they can get through."

Laughter comes from the small crowd inside the square. "Tell them to go around," someone shouts.

"Go around," the Snyman boy shouts from the top of the harvester. He listens to the blacks' reply and reports back. "They say it will take too long. If they can't go through the square they have to go back to the station and across the river by the old bridge. They'll be late for work."

Jannie Malan of Ouklip jumps onto the harvester with the Snyman boy. "Since when do they care about being late for work?" he shouts. He waves a fist at the blacks and points out the way around the circle of farm machinery with a stainless steel bull castrator. People laugh and shout and honk their horns. A young man near them pounds the back of his tiller with a spade, and other people take up the rhythm, beating faster and faster against their machines with tools or fists. Suddenly they stop. Heila sees the Snyman boy has his arms out for silence like Dominee when he pronounces the blessing. He speaks in a church voice: "They have decided to go around." Everyone cheers and laughs, and the noise starts up all over again.

On the other end of the square a policemen is shouting through a loud hailer for *them* to disperse. "You are obstructing the traffic," he says.

"De Klerk is obstructing us," someone shouts. "Give us de Klerk. We want to talk to de Klerk."

"I have an interdict," the policeman shouts. He waves a piece of paper. "From Pretoria. Right from the top. You have ten minutes to start moving your machines."

Jannie Malan waves his castrator above his head. "We don't want your interdick. It's de Klerk's dick we want." Heila laughs like everyone else.

For the next ten minutes the people wait about to see what the police will do. They tell stories to keep themselves angry. "They're getting cheekier every day," someone says. "They don't even wait till you're out of the car before they steal it anymore. They know de Klerk's going to let Mandela out."

Someone else is telling about his vacation in Durban. "Never again, I said to Milly," he says. "The beaches are filth. Hardly a white face to be seen. They've taken over. We saw it ourselves, didn't we Milly. They just do their business right there on the beach, like dogs."

"Fanus has a cat that goes to the toilet," Heila says. She is thinking of Kay and May's new beau at the retirement center. His cat drinks water from the tap and squats on the toilet to do its business. Fanus plays his guitar at Kay's window one night and at May's the next, after the eight o'clock news. Then they go over to his flat to see his cat's tricks. Fanus has a box of cookies made especially for cats. The cookies are shaped like fishes. After the cat performs on the toilet, Fanus holds a cookie between his teeth by its fish tail for the cat to take. Heila thinks of Kay and May laughing, looking at each other, not having to speak, because they are twins and know each other's thoughts. And Heila, the older sister, has always been jealous that she did not have someone like that. Once, for a while, she thought she had. But all her life she has been the one who got things last and had them taken away first.

Heila must have been five, six, when Maria came to live with them. Orphaned in the coolie flu of '27. "A twin for you," Ma said, although the girl she nudged into the bedroom was a head taller than Heila. Heila did not care. She made up a story about herself and Maria just like the one about Kay and May who had fitted into a tomato box next to the stove, and Ma having to hold up a feather to their noses to see if they were still breathing. "Look the other way," Maria said before undressing every night. Once the candle was out, they talked, just like Kay and May in the other bed.

Palace, house, hovel, pig sty. To see what love would bring them, she and Maria and Kay and May used to count off like that: the kernels on their corn-on-the-cob, the pips in their oranges, the buttons on Mr. Faure's waistcoats when he started courting Maria. When the people at Maria's funeral said, "She's with her Savior" to comfort Heila, all she could think was that Maria would not care for heaven unless Jesus too turned out to wear fancy waistcoats.

What love brought Heila was Jacobus Kloppers.

On the day after Karl Meyer had left for Germany to fetch his bride, Heila did not get up to go to work. She stayed in bed with the covers over her head. Ma came in and sat by her feet. Heila could smell the camphor on Ma's hands as she rubbed and rubbed Heila's legs through the blankets. She thought she knew what Ma was going to say. *Better to know him for what he is now than when it is too late.* But Ma did not say it. Instead she did something that surprised Heila. Ma had never approved of her job at Mukherjee's store. It was no place for a white woman. But on that day Ma got Heila ready to go. She brought a basin of water and a cloth, and washed Heila like a corpse. She dressed her and combed her hair. She took her hand and walked with her until they were past the watchmaker's shop. Then Heila came to herself, and told Ma she could go home.

At the store she went to the back to see what had come on the train overnight. She levered open the crate, and bent her cheek down to feel the knobbly texture of the wedding dress lace from Holland. With an armful of rolled guipure she halted in front of the bolts of seersucker puckered like foreheads, and asked them for a sign. Jacobus walked in. What she took as a confirmation that he was the one was that he, too, took an hour to select a few purchases. Only what he was buying was nails, salt, and dip. And what he gave her, when he got around to proposing, was a roll of red flannel that lasted until after the boys went to boarding school and would no longer wear the pajamas she used it to make.

Jacobus's thin voice comes from the center of a group of people. "De Klerk wants to take everything from us and give it to them," he says. "Why can't they work for their own things? Things didn't grow on my back. I worked hard for everything I have. I'll fight for it. It won't be the first time." Heila knows the story he is going to tell. With every telling the number of shots he fired at the Land Bank officials' jeep gets greater. What he won't tell is what *he* took away from *her*: he cheated on her! Heila wants Jacobus to look at her so she can turn her face away, but he is absorbed in his story. The young men are egging him on. "So what did you do then, oom Jacobus?" Jacobus's voice gets louder from the attention.

A roar starts up in Heila's head. She looks at the sky, but there are only a few clouds. Then she sees it is not only her. People are turning to each other to ask what is going on. They run to the edge of the barricade to see. Jacobus trots a few yards behind the young men, looking like one of Ouma Mave's monster babies with his spindly legs. *Wring his neck and dump him on the deck, stomp on his head and he'll be dead.* How little Maidie used to wiggle her little bottom and stamp her feet when Heila sang this song to her.

The Snyman boy's wife tries to give Heila a hand up onto the truck bed where they are all standing, but it is too high. "Never mind," Heila says. She leans against one of the big tires and peers through the bottom. A phalanx of tanks, just like those you see on TV keeping the peace in the townships, is crawling toward the wall of farm machinery. Their brown and green camouflage makes them stand out against the black of the road. They are called Caspirs, Heila remembers. Their noise swallows up the shouts and the scuffle of shoes above Heila's head. She holds her breath, waiting for the sound to peak.

One of the Caspirs is making straight for Heila. When its gun is almost touching the truck, it stops. A soldier stands up inside it and tells the people to move away from the vehicles so that the personnel can do their work.

An angry cry goes up from all over the square.

Young boys, like Frederik's Fred who's in the army, climb out of the Caspir. *This thing in our nation has set brother against brother and father against son.* They start looking for places to hook chains onto the Snyman boy's nice red harvester. One of them loops a chain around the front axle, but before he can hook it up, the Snyman boy jumps from the truck and pulls it free. He scuffles with the young soldier who tries to get back his hook. Other farmers jump in to help.

From underneath the truck Heila sees Jacobus climbing up the steps of the Snyman boy's harvester. With every step his ridiculous little behind bobs backward, and at the bottom of his pants a piece of white leg shows above the top of his socks. He gets into the cab and starts up the harvester. "Hook her up," he shouts to the Snyman boy. "We'll see who pulls who."

"Go for it, oom Jacobus." One of the hooks takes, and the chain tautens under the pull of the two vehicles. The harvester lurches forward, pulling the Caspir along a few feet. Cheers of support go up for the harvester. It comes to Heila that Jacobus might hurt himself. She has to stop him. Making a fool of himself in front of the young people just so he can make another story out of it. She won't have it. Anger tightens her throat, so her shouts come out with no sound. She runs from under the truck and goes after Jacobus. She won't let him do it. If he hurts himself, how will she leave him? How will she get away from the loneliness, from the farm, from the work he'll make? Oh, he'd love being an invalid. Heila, fetch this. Heila, scratch here. She won't let him. She'll move into the place by Kay and May, by Fanus with his cat. Always someone *there* to talk to.

A shot rings out and Jacobus tumbles from the cab clutching his arm. He rolls and rolls until he is right at Heila's feet. A red petunia, like the ones in Kay and May's window box, opens up on his shirtsleeve.

Heila kneels down and clutches his hand. A little high wail comes from her mouth.

"Do something, Heila," Jacobus says.

That's what he said to her that first time the river was in spate and the water came up to the kitchen and floated the firewood around the legs of her new slow combustion. *Heila, do something.* While the water was going down, he sat on a kitchen chair on top of the kitchen table with the account books while she swept and wrung and hung things out to dry. Telling the story on himself in company to make it sound like a joke. *Such a card, oom Jacobus.*

The Snyman boy kneels over Jacobus. "The buggers," he says. "Shooting at their own people." He pulls Jacobus's shirt off his shoulder with a tug that snaps off a button and sends it whizzing past Heila's face. He wipes away the blood with his handkerchief. Only a little new blood wells up. It is only a nick.

The thumping going on in Heila's chest slows down.

"The bank," she says. "Doctor Taylor will have to tie up that arm before we can go to the bank."

Jacobus looks the other way. "I don't want Doctor Taylor," he says in his crotchety voice. "I want Hennie."

Heila takes his head between her hands and makes him look at her. "You know Hennie is in Pretoria," she says. "Doctor Taylor can phone him. He can tell Doctor Taylor what to put on."

A soldier is kneeling by Jacobus. "We'll have a medic check that at the police station."

Other soldiers gather around them. Heila sits a minute watching the khaki shorts with hairy knees dangling from them all around her. Under her green town dress her own legs feel like hoses with the water let out of them.

Jacobus sits up. "I won't let just any doctor touch me," he says. "My son is a doctor. My wife will call him to look at it."

The soldier looks at Heila.

"We can't go to the police station," Heila says. "I have to go to the bank. We are going to visit my sisters. Their beau has a cat that uses the toilet."

The first soldier speaks sternly to Jacobus. "Shame on you for bringing the auntie to this place. She's in shock."

"No," Jacobus says. "It's not shock. It's her mind. Some days she's mixed up. What does she want to go to the bank for? What do you want to go to the bank for, Heila? You don't have any money in the bank. You signed it over, for the tractor. Remember?"

Anger and shame swirl white and pink in Heila's head. She does not remember. She signed a paper, but he said it was so the tractor could be in her name also. She would never have signed over her money. He is just saying this to humiliate her. There is nothing wrong with her head. He has to make out that she is mixed up because of what she does remember: that when he cheated on her it wasn't even with a white woman. She could tell the police about it right now. They'd arrest him. Miscegenation is against the law.

"You take her straight home," the soldier says. He is tying the Snyman boy's handkerchief around Jacobus's arm. "This is no place for you."

Two other soldiers are putting handcuffs on the Snyman boy. Other farmers are being led away. Some are being pulled, leaving a green wake where their shoes drag against the nap of the lawn.

Their soldier helps them to their feet.

"He can't take *me* home," Heila says. "I have to take *him* home. He failed his driver's license."

The soldier walks them to their tractor, holding Heila by the elbow like a father giving his daughter away in marriage. He helps her into the cab. He helps her find the keys in her handbag. Jacobus is getting in on the other side.

Heila starts up the engine. The soldier wags his hand for her to follow him. He walks ahead of the tractor, showing her with the air between his palms how much space she has to get past the Snyman boy's harvester. When they get to the side street, he waves good-bye.

"Your flicker, Heila," Jacobus says. "The yellow thing by the wheel."

"I know," Heila says. She remembers. Her hands know where to go. Names she forgets, and sometimes the date. Or what side of the road to drive on when she is very tired. She waits for a moving blur on the road to turn into a car, and when it has rumbled by, she pulls in behind it. She lines up the bull on the tractor's hood with the white dashes on the road like Frederik has taught her. After a while it is hard to see the road. Large raindrops are making muddy splats on the dusty cab window.

She was ten when it rained so much that a foot of water ran over the storm water bridge across the drift. Ma sent down Needle the yard boy, wrapped in a clean sheet, to fetch them across after school. How Kay and May shrieked, and Maria, who by then was fourteen and bigger than Ma. How Heila clung to Needle's back when her turn came, with her legs pressed into his sides and her hands digging into his shoulders. The water swirling below and the bitter smell of his sweat right under her nose.

When they got home, a flock of tick-birds was bogged down between the orchard rows, each bird highstepping on blobs of clay stuck to its feet. She and Kay and May caught them, with their school socks pulled over their hands against the lashing beaks. They lifted the birds into the empty water trough. So much wildness gathered in a small place. Before they could agree on a plan for their rescue, the water gathering in the trough's bottom had washed the birds clean. One by one they shook themselves and took off with a whoosh. It was when Heila went inside to dry herself off that she happened upon Maria squatting on the floor, scraping herself down there with a number two crotchet hook. All that night Maria screamed into the pillow. A warm wetness came from her side of the bed onto Heila's night-dress. Heila knew that was how babies came out, and was terri-fied something might be alive in the bed. But in the morning there was only Maria, dead, and no feather needed to test the stillness round her open mouth. It was not until Heila started her own monthly sickness two years later that she asked Ma why Maria didn't just marry Mr. Faure. "Mr. Faure," Ma said, surprised. "If only it had been Mr. Faure. No, Heila, it was much worse. It was Needle. I found them in the milk room, that day it rained so much. And although she denied it, it wasn't the first time either. She was four months gone, at least. Maria made her bed—and I'll say this for her: she chose the only way there was to sleep in it."

Heila too has made her bed. From the tractor's other seat Jacobus is telling her what to do.

"The wipers, Heila," Jacobus says. "The knob with the mustache."

"I know," Heila says. Always bossing her. Proving things. That they made a mistake with the eye test. That she is the one who cannot see things. But she sees everything. Except who she can believe when they tell her something. She should have known. Jacobus wanting to put the tractor in her name! Since when did he ever want to give her anything? When little Maidie was born, he did not even put her birth in the paper. The boys' announcements he put in. But little Maidie he only put in the paper when she died.

When they come to the old bridge near the station Heila has to slow down. Black people are blocking the way. Umbrellas and plastic bags held over their heads form a moving roof over the road. More blacks are sheltering under the bridge on the riverbank. They are backed up all the way to the railway lines.

"Just keep going, Heila," Jacobus says. "They'll get out of the way. Put it in low. Don't scrape the clutch. Give it some gas."

Heila feels confused. Jacobus makes her confused. Being bossy. Not like Frederik. Frederik tells her one thing at a time. She'll ignore Jacobus, do it her own way. Her foot pushes down on the gas a little too hard. The tractor lurches forward. Over the engine's roar she can hear the people on the bridge shouting. They run for the guardrails and flatten themselves against them. A path opens up for the tractor. In the middle of the path a child stands with its arms outstretched. Heila pulls at the steering wheel. The tractor turns sideways. She tries to find the brake.

When the bull on the hood already hangs in the blue sky above the river, her foot picks out the right pedal. The tractor stops. The child hasn't budged. It sticks out its tongue, as if tasting the rain.

"Don't stop, Heila. Turn around. Give it gas. Keep going."

The sun breaks through the clouds. Rain diamonds glitter on the windshield wipers. "It's a jackal's wedding," Heila says. That's what you say when it rains when the sun shines. *Mohammed ate a pig.* That's what you shout when you walk past Mukherjee's shop.

The child clambers up the tractor's hood and presses its face against the window glass. A globule of rain skambles down the glass onto its squashed black nose. Heila laughs. Not black. Pink holes with brown around it. Heila thinks of little Maidie. Her skin so white, Mrs. Brummer used to say she was an angel dropped from heaven. *Barefoot baby, where did you / get those lovely eyes of blue?* Heila opens her handbag. She wants to find her savings book. She tugs at the window catch with one hand.

"Don't open the window, Heila." Jacobus's voice is a high whine. "Keep going, Heila. They kill old people. You're forgetting."

No. Heila does not forget. She remembers. She remembers the woman who came to the kitchen door on the day she got back on her feet after birthing Maidie. The woman was black, but the child tied to her back was a light brown. Its eyes were blue. The woman wanted money, she said. From the child's father. Or she would go to the police. Heila wanted to laugh. She told the woman she was crazy. *Heila* was the one who was going to go to the police. But then she saw Jacobus. He had come into the kitchen. He was deathly white, as if *he* had just given birth. He sat down at the table and covered his face with his hands. *Heila.* That time he said please. *Please please. Forgive me.*

Heila did something. She gathered up some of the things she had knitted and sewed for little Maidie, and some of the boys' things, and even one of her own dresses. She bundled it all in the yard or two of red flannel she still had left on the roll. The woman would not take it. She wanted money. "We don't have money," Heila said. She pointed to the newspaper on the table. "Look. We did not even have money to put the baby in the paper." When she said that, Jacobus left the kitchen. A few minutes later he was back. His hands were fisted around bundles of money. Paper money. More than Heila had ever seen. He threw the notes at the woman. Some of them swooped right down, others fluttered to the floor with a zigzag motion. The woman stooped to pick them up. Each time she bent down the baby on her back lurched forward, so Heila thought it might fall out of its blanket and dash its head on the hard cement. She wished it would, she will now admit. Then, though, she did not yet know what it was to see a child dead.

In the tractor next to Heila Jacobus is saying please again. Please put in the clutch, please turn the key, please start it up. Heila will, as soon as the child is off the hood. He is sliding down now. He squats on the ground, grinning up at her. She rolls down the window. She finds some pennies in her bag and tosses them. They catch the sun as they spiral down. The child stretches out his arm as if to catch the coins in the air. The tractor's huge front windshield blossoms white. Tiny cubes of glass tinkle into Heila's lap. Rocks thudding on the cab roof make a bigger sound. One whirrs by Heila's head and hits Jacobus's door with a clunk. Somebody is breaking Jacobus's window with the point of an umbrella.

Heila remembers how to put the tractor in reverse. Jacobus is not telling her what to do. He is hugging his arms over his chest. Heila presses her foot against the gas. Her legs feel strong, like a young woman standing on tiptoe to kiss her beau.

The tractor jerks into motion. The tops of heads bob forward past Heila's window. There is a jolt, and the tractor slows down. A woman wearing a floral head scarf runs up and starts climbing up the cab steps. When her head is level with Heila's, Heila steps down on the gas. The woman falls away. There is a tearing, cracking noise. A piece of the bridge railing flies past the window. The back of the tractor lifts, then dips. Outside, people are screaming. The steering wheel spins by itself under Heila's hands. Then she herself slides without effort across the seat toward Jacobus. For a moment they are huddled like twins in his corner.

"Kay and May have a new kind of petunia," Heila tells Jacobus. His lips open and close, but she can't hear him over the noise that fills the cab. It sounds like a thousand farmers are scraping their rakes and hoes along the side of the tractor.

Heila shouts louder. "It's white, with just a dusting of yellow. It's called *Angel's Breath*."

The front end of the cab seesaws up. Jacobus's startled face moves slowly toward Heila. His mouth is like a baby's when you ask it how the piggy goes.

Heila looks past Jacobus out his window. An eye-blue sky smudged with cloud is streaking past. In the outside mirror, the river sage is rushing toward her. Its sweet, sweet smell is making her heady. She feels her old life untacking itself from her skin, billowing behind her with the silken rustle of a petticoat in the breeze.

"Have you ever?" she says. "Such a name for a flower."

Pig Day

This could be a birthday sleepover. In the moonglow of the streetlamp through the window anyone could be the lump in the other sleeping bag. Anyone. The mummied legs lifting into a pup tent next to the couch could be Nick's. Nick's eyes could be behind the hair spilled forward like a wing across the face. In this sliver of wakefulness Jared doesn't want to be sure. He lets the doubt fog around him, sinks into the drugged possibility that what has happened for real is really a nightmare.

So in the morning the lump is not Nick, but Mihalik, who groans and coughs and snorts open his nose. It is Mihalik who krrrtses open the zipper and bumps the couch when he gets up and scuffles barefoot to the kitchen. Mihalik is Nick's father. Mihalik is his last name, but that's what Nick calls him. When Mihalik went to Romania to fetch Nick from his mother he was already almost six and too big to get into the habit of saying "Dad."

Jared opens his eyes and checks his watch. Seventeen hours

have passed. Nick is dead. Last night Jared knew the fact of it before the green sheet over Nick's face, before the paramedics, even before the ambulance. He knew because three things had come together in an acute triangle in his chest: the surprising smell of firecrackers, Nick slumping in slow motion like a joke from the back of the truck onto the driveway, and the weight of Mihalik's hunting rifle pivoting by the trigger guard from his, Jared's, own fingers. He had known even before Mihalik, with blood on his beard from trying to blow life into Nick's mouth like God, said: "Jesus fucking Christ. You killed him."

Mihalik squats by Jared's sleeping bag with a cup of coffee and holds it to his face. The smell forces him to open his eyes. "We have work to do, Bud," Mihalik says.

Mihalik doesn't call people Bud. He calls them Jerk or Shithead or Asshole. He sometimes calls Nick worse things than that. A few weeks ago he called him Vojodusu. That was after Nick and Jared took Mihalik's truck to go practice up the canyon for when they would get their driver's permits next semester. Mihalik was supposed to be upstairs for the night with one of his women, but somehow he noticed that they had taken a couple of beers from the fridge and that the truck was gone. He called the cops and had them arrested when they drove back down. When the cops called Mihalik to release them to his custody, Mihalik would not take them back. So the boys slept on the sheriff's living room floor in sleeping bags the sheriff had brought over from the jail. Mihalik did give them a ride home the next morning when he came over to fetch his truck. "Do you want to kill yourself?" he shouted in Nick's face when he picked them up at the jail. "Vojodusu." Nick hadn't known exactly what it meant, even though he'd been born in Romania. He just knew it was bad, worse than motherfucker, because Mihalik had called him that before. Jared and Nick liked the sound of this new word. They spray painted it across the tenth-grade lockers one night after school although they didn't know how it was spelled.

Jared slurps coffee to rinse his mouth. He doesn't drink coffee. He doesn't drink vodka either, but he did last night. At first Mihalik made him, then he had wanted to. He would have finished the bottle if Mihalik hadn't taken it away. Mihalik calls from the kitchen that breakfast is ready. Jared kicks off the sleeping bag and sits down to a plate of bacon and eggs and toast. "Eat," Mihalik says.

Between Jared's teeth the egg suddenly feels like one of Nick's ears, or his tongue, which by now is cold as meat in the mortuary refrigerator. Jared holds a dishrag to his mouth and knocks over a chair on his way to the bathroom. He turns on the shower with one hand so Mihalik won't hear him throw up. When there's nothing left in his stomach, he gets in under the spray and lets the cold water trickle through his shirt and pants, lets it drip from his balls and cock shrunk up tight against his body. When he thinks that if he can only stand the cold a bit longer he'll be dead like Nick, Mihalik is in the doorway holding out a towel and a handful of Nick's clothes. Jared dries himself and puts on Nick's underwear and shorts and his Love Comes in Spurts T-shirt.

"Do you have a suit?" Mihalik says.

"No," Jared says. He combs his hair with his fingers. Nick keeps a comb on him. A pink see-through comb with glitter embedded in the plastic. Becky Miller won it in Holey-Moley on tenth-grade Fun Day. On the way back in the bus she tried to comb Nick's hair with it and he wrestled it away from her.

"We'll have to get you a suit," Mihalik says. "We have many things to do."

Jared does not know how it is possible to do things. But Mihalik is in a hurry and Jared follows him to his workshop, listening to the order of business. The first thing Mihalik and Jared do on this morning after is to pack an order of Mihalik's trinket boxes for a gift shop in Yellowstone. The boxes are works of art, the tag that Jared has to stick on each box says. They don't look like trinket boxes, they look like odd-shaped pieces of wood. Only if you look closely and push the right spot in the back does a tiny drawer pop out of the polished wood surface.

Jared does what he knows is Nick's job. He wraps each box in bubble plastic and places it in a cardboard box. When the box is too full for another layer, Mihalik tells him to stuff the space at the top with more plastic. He shoots the lid tight with a stapling gun. While Mihalik does the paperwork for UPS, Jared loads ten signposts that Mihalik has made for Doan's Real Estate onto the truck. Jared manages to do this without looking at the place on the driveway where the night before Mrs. Tilgman from next door scrubbed every trace of Nick's blood as soon as the police would let her. As he watched the beams from the headlights of the sheriff's car catch and let go of Mrs. Tilgman's swaying behind, Jared thought for the first time of how it would be to tell his mother. It was Thursday. Her early night. She would have been home since four from her job at the nursery. Would she be storytelling drunk, or sullen drunk, or passed out drunk? He'd lost track of the time.

"Will you tell my mother?" he asked the sheriff. The sheriff was leaning on his car, waiting for Mrs. Tilgman to finish, waiting to give Jared a ride home.

"She's going to take it bad," Jared said. He knew that the sheriff knew what that meant. Once before, when he'd thought someone had done something bad to his mother, he'd had to call the cops. It turned out that what was wrong with his mother she'd done to herself. She'd been mad at the man who called to say they were coming to take back the furniture. So she'd cut open a couch cushion and pulled out some stuffing and then later had fallen asleep on top of it naked, too drunk to take care of her period.

Jared puts the last signpost on top of the others. As it turned out, he did not go home the night before. He is still here, although Nick's yard looks different today. The world looks different. Jared doesn't remember the sun ever being so bright, or seeing a pink quite like the one Mihalik has used to paint the signposts. He is sure he will remember this moment forever: the tingle of sun heat on his scalp, the defeated angle of Mihalik's back as he sets the box on the front steps for the UPS man. They get into the truck.

"Can we go by my house?" Jared asks.

"Sure," Mihalik says.

"I need some stuff," Jared says. He tells Mihalik where to go. They stop in front of the house. Jared isn't sure about just arriving, even though Mihalik had called last night to make sure the sheriff had told his mother. He wishes Mihalik would go inside with him, but doesn't know how to ask. So it is a relief when Mihalik gets out of the truck by himself and goes up to the door with him. He holds his breath until they're inside, but it looks good. The place is picked up. His mother is pale and sober. She is clean. Her hair is still wet from a shower and sticks in drippy tangles to the freckled piece of her shoulders that shows from her blouse. She cries when she hugs him.

"It's going to be okay," she says. She shakes Mihalik's hand and squeezes his arm. "So sorry for your loss," she says.

Jared looks at his mother amazed. Sometimes she knows things to say. Once, when he was in sixth grade, she came to parent-teacher conference. She wore a nice blue dress with white dots and a white collar. She sat on one of the small chairs on one side of the desk. Miss Turner sent Jared across the room for his decorated folder of work, and when he turned back he saw them talking together. For a moment he thought, You can't tell who's the mother and who's the teacher.

"Thank you," Mihalik says to Jared's mother. "What's happened has happened. Now we do what we have to do, that's what counts."

"If there's anything I can do," Jared's mother says.

"If I have your permission," Mihalik says, "I'd like Jared to be with me a while longer."

"Anything I can do to make this time easier for you, Mr. Mihalik," Jared's mother says.

"Jozef," Mihalik says.

Jared's mother says to call her Melinda. "It's a pity we didn't get to know each other in happier circumstances," she says. "Of course I knew Nick. They were such good friends, your boy and my Jared."

The air grows too heavy to breathe in the room where Jared had always been afraid to bring Nick because he hadn't known what he would find there when he opened the front door. Jared goes to his room. It looks the same. The road signs he and Nick have pried off their posts from all over the neighborhood this summer block the same geometrical patches of faded floral wallpaper. They keep the signs here, so Mihalik will not find out. He'd probably make a citizen's arrest if he knew. That's what Nick told Jared, because he was afraid to take his share of the collection to his house. Jared likes their rusty smell, their tidy shapes. Pi r squared, he thinks about the stop sign before he falls asleep at night. Half base times height is the yield sign from the intersection near the school. Length times width is the "No Trespassing" from the private road up the canyon. Now Jared sits with his back against the wall, his legs straight on the bed making a right angle. The square on the hypotenuse equals the sum of the squares on the other two sides.

Jared's mother comes to tell him that Mihalik wants to go.

She sits next to him and holds his hand. "You don't have to go with him if you don't want to," she says. "I will buy you a suit. We don't have to look other people in the eye. I'm going to be here for you."

Jared remembers something that happened in third grade. He had just come home from school one afternoon. A kid across the road was swinging a cat in circles by the hind legs. Some other kids were counting the revolutions. When they got to twenty, the kid stopped and put the cat down. It crawled on its belly for a while, then got to its feet and staggered into the road. Jared, who was watching from the window, felt his mother's warm, fruity breath on his neck. When one of the kids caught the cat again before it got too sure on its feet, his mother opened the window. "You can't do that to a cat," she shouted.

"I can," the boy said. "It's mine."

Jared's mother moved fast then. She took a handful of money from the Tampax box where she kept her drinking fund. She marched out the door and lurched toward the kids in the street.

"That cat is not yours," she said to the boy. She was careful of the way she said her s's.

"It is," he said. He looked scared. Jared's mother could be magnificent when she was drunk.

"How much did you pay for him?" she asked.

"A—a dollar," the boy said. Anyone could see he was making it up.

"I'll give you five," Jared's mother said. She counted off five dollars into his shirt pocket and took the cat from his arms. She brought it into their house. She put it on the carpet and they watched it. For the rest of the afternoon they fed it half-and-half and a whole can of tuna. The next day it was gone.

Jared's mother rubs the hairs on his arm, which are reddish like hers. Jared thinks of the night before. When the sheriff was ready to take Jared home, he shook Mihalik's hand and told him again that there probably wouldn't be any charges. Jared stood by the cop car ready to get in, but when Mihalik turned his back and walked toward the house, Jared remembered what he had said through his beard flamed with blood: "You killed him." He remembered it despite the fact that Mihalik had taken the blame on himself when the cops came, saying like he'd always said before taking them shooting, "A loaded gun is the owner's responsibility." Jared felt as if his hand that had pulled the trigger and Mihalik's hand that had not taken the bullet out of the chamber were handcuffed together. That was when he asked the sheriff to go tell his mother. He, Jared, followed Mihalik inside.

Jared pulls his hand out from under his mother's and sits forward on the bed. "Do you still have that blue dress with the white collar?" he asks.

"I never had a dress with a white collar," she says. "It's not my style. But I'll find something nice for the funeral. I won't embarrass you."

At the funeral home Jared waits in the reception cubicle while Delia takes Mihalik to the back to see Nick. Delia Bjorkman was his soccer coach in elementary school, and owns the mortuary. Although she is wearing a grey suit now, he can see that her thighs are just as thick as they used to be in her coaching shorts. He's not sure she remembers him. He has changed. After a few minutes she comes back. They sit down in sky-blue upholstered chairs with gold trim. "Do you still play soccer?" she asks. When he says no, she asks him how long he's known Nick, and then runs out of things to say. She hands him a brochure with a pen sketch of Bjorkman's Funeral Home on the outside. Her signature in round letters is hidden in the shrubs by the front door.

"Mr. Mihalik tells me you are going to help him decide on the options," she says.

"I guess." Jared glances through the brochure. Color photographs show what you get for each price. There are white coffins for babies. There's pink or blue with stuffed patchwork bears in the lid for toddlers. There's light wood with pleated pink or white satin for women. There's dark wood with red or royal blue or tartan for men. Silk or velvet. Gold or silver trim. When Jared is through, he flicks the pages with his thumb. All the options blend into one coffin which jumps about on the page.

Mihalik appears outside the glass window of the cubicle. He wipes his eyes on his T-shirt sleeve before coming in. He sits in the other blue chair. He covers his eyes with one hand. Delia leans over and pats his other hand. She passes him a tissue box covered in the same material as the chairs. He pushes it away. "I'm okay," he says. "Let's get down to business."

They go through the brochure.

"The price includes use of chapel and limousine for mourners," Delia says.

Mihalik asks Jared: red or blue lining, gold or silver trim, matte or gloss finish. Mihalik chooses, Jared says, sure. Delia goes through the choices for the flowers. "It's included," she says.

"I want to see it," Mihalik says when Jared thinks they're done.

"I don't have the flowers," Delia says. "We get them fresh on the day."

"I want to see the coffin," Mihalik says.

Delia is flustered. "I don't keep them either," she says. "People usually just choose from the pictures. I'll phone in your order and my representative will have it here in time for the viewing on Sunday."

"Paper is patient," Mihalik says.

Delia looks puzzled.

"Romanian proverb," Mihalik says. "I want to see it."

Delia shakes her head. "It's not really professional, I suppose, but I can let you see someone else's that's almost the same."

They follow Delia into the viewing room. Between two upright stands of flowers an old woman lies in a coffin of light brown wood. She wears a powder blue dress and in her hands she holds a lace handkerchief. Jared thinks of Nick. He hopes Delia won't make Nick hold a handkerchief. Nick would look fucking ridiculous holding a handkerchief.

Mihalik is stroking the wood.

"Birch," Delia says. "Our most popular light."

"Ash," Mihalik says. "And the finish is shoddy. Bubbles. They did not sand between applications."

Delia looks shocked. "I'm sorry, Mr. Mihalik. No one's ever said anything. I'll talk to my representative. I can guarantee yours will be top quality."

"You're not going to put anything in Nick's hands, are you?" Jared asks.

"We covered that under options," Delia says. "Usually the girls have flowers and the boys have a book. The other day I did a boy with a baseball mitt. Of course it's the parents' option to leave it in or take it out before the interment as a keepsake."

"Can't he just hold nothing?" Jared says. "He would like to hold nothing. What's fucking wrong with holding nothing?" Hot needles sting his eyes and he runs into the reception cubicle. When he looks back through the glass panel, the viewing room is distant as a description in a book. What brings it back to real life is Mihalik's angry voice.

"Their effing mortises are too shallow," Mihalik shouts. He is bending over the woman in the coffin to examine the hinges on the lid. "The top's not flush."

"We have to vacate the room," Delia says. She leads Mihalik away by the elbow. "Their preview is in a few minutes."

"Butt joints," Mihalik says. "Fucking butt joints."

Back in the reception cubicle, Mihalik looks as if he suddenly remembers where he is. He steps toward the wall and takes a close-up look at a painting of a sky-blue ocean topped with gold-trimmed clouds. "Nice," he says.

"I dabble, Mr. Mihalik," Delia says. "In my spare time."

"Jozef," Mihalik says. "Call me Jozef."

When they get back to Mihalik's house with their new suits

on hangers, Mrs. Tilgman from next door stands waiting with a fruit pie bubbling red syrup through the holes in the crust. She also brings over flowers and cards that have arrived during the morning. A large manila envelope from the school has a computer-printed banner that says "We Love You, Nick." It is signed by everyone in the tenth grade. Mrs. Tilgman tapes it to the strip of wall above the kitchen cupboards while Mihalik and Jared eat her pie.

When Jared is done, he takes his suit to Nick's bedroom. Nick's computer is playing the demonstration program of Nick's favorite game over and over again. It is on from the day before, from before they got in the truck to go try out Mihalik's new clay-pigeon launcher. Jared drops the suit on the bed and sits down. He watches the movement of the shapes on the screen.

Jared types in the start command and starts playing. He fits in half a wall of tiles. He hears Mihalik behind him. He misses. His score flashes on the screen. Above it, it says, All-time Winner: NICK.

Mihalik sits down on Nick's bed next to the new suit. Tears run across the pink around his eyes and into his beard. A high wail comes from his mouth.

Jared runs from the sound. He runs into the sitting room where his sleeping bag is still lying on the floor from the night before. He crawls into it and pulls the flap up over his head. Still, the sound comes through the Quallofill and through his skin and into the place in his stomach that still feels hungry although he's eaten half of Mrs. Tilgman's pie.

When it goes quiet, Jared feels like he did in the ringing silence after the shot. It seems that if he could just concentrate he would know the answer to something distant and profound. But then the noise starts up again. Only this time the wail that fills the hollows of his bones is coming from Mihalik's electric saw. Jared strips off the sleeping bag and goes across the backyard to the workshop. Mihalik shouts something over the whine of the machine. Jared can't hear what it is, but he can see that the end of the long board coming through the saw should be held by someone. He walks closer and supports the warm weight of it with both hands.

They work on Nick's coffin all night. They cut the boards from walnut posts that Mihalik salvaged from a torn-down building years before.

"This is the good stuff," Mihalik says. He runs his hand over each piece after they cut it. "You can't buy stuff like this today. No knots. No sap pockets."

"These four joined shiplapped for the front, and the same for the back," Mihalik says. He measures and marks the pieces. He writes front, side, bottom or back on each piece. He sets up the router and rabbets the edges. He shouts instructions to Jared. "Not so much glue," he says. "The glue will stick to itself and not to the wood."

"Butt joints," Mihalik says. He spits it out like one of his swearwords. "Not on anything of mine. Dovetail joints. I'm making dovetail joints for Nick."

Nick wouldn't know the difference between a dovetail and a butt, Jared thinks. But he doesn't say anything. He thinks of the sound that might come out of Mihalik's mouth if he stops talking about what his hands are doing.

When the sun rises on Saturday morning, the box is clamped and they have to wait for the glue to dry. Mihalik starts measuring out the lid. Jared is tired and hungry. He goes over to the house and makes French toast and coffee. When it is done, he calls Mihalik from the workshop. Mihalik goes to the bathroom, and doesn't come back. When Jared looks for him, he finds him asleep on the couch. Jared eats the French toast and drinks the coffee. He lies on Nick's bed and sleeps.

It is afternoon and Delia is coming over. Mihalik has called her to explain the change in plans. He still wants to use the chapel and limousine, he has told her, but he's bringing his own coffin. She is upset, Mihalik says. She is expecting a big turnout at the viewing. They had a nice write-up on Nick in the paper, she said. On the front page. She asked if they had seen it. Mihalik said no, they'd been busy sanding.

Jared's hair and clothes are covered in dust. Mihalik tells Jared to keep sanding. "With the grain," he says as he leaves the workshop. When he comes back, he has showered and changed. He has brought along a roll of gift paper and wraps one of his trinket boxes.

Delia finds them in the workshop. She is wearing an apricot-colored skirt with a coordinated top, and white sandals. The skirt makes her hips look enormous. She comes right up to Jared. "May I hug you?" she says. She doesn't wait for him to answer. Her close-up smell is damp and flowery.

"How are you?" Mihalik says to Delia as if he really wants to know. He gives her the box.

"For me?" she says. She blushes. She unwraps it. "It's beautiful."

Mihalik shows her the place in the back to push. He shows her the inside of the drawer lined with velvet. He touches her shoulder while he tells her about the Yellowstone order. He goes over to the coffin. "That's what this will look like when it's done," he says.

Delia doesn't say anything.

"I knew you'd understand," Mihalik says. "You're an artist too—your painting."

Jared moves his sanding block to and fro. He remembers to go with the grain.

It is Sunday morning. Jared is rubbing resin oil into the coffin. It is the third application. The wood looks rich and old like a gunstock shiny with the oil of many hands.

Mihalik comes back from the house with a beer for each of them. He sits on a stool on the other side. He is working on the lid. "Wood will do pretty much what you want it to," he says.

"I guess," Jared says.

"In Japan they have these temples that are thousands of years old," Mihalik says. "But actually they aren't. They break them down and build them from scratch every forty years or so."

"When were you in Japan?" Jared says to say something.

"I wasn't," Mihalik says. "I read it in a woodwork book."

"What does Vojodusu mean?" Jared says.

Mihalik stops rubbing. He fixes his eyes on the tools hanging behind Jared on the wall. "It's a bad word," he says. "You can only say it to someone once in your life. And it has to be someone you love."

Jared tries to imagine a place where there are rules for swearwords. "What was it like, living in Romania?"

"It means 'you fucked with my soul,'" Mihalik says.

There is such a thick quiet around Mihalik that Jared thinks about a woman he saw on TV who could break a glass with her voice. When Mihalik starts talking again he speaks so softly Jared has to lean forward to hear. "There is a story my mother used to tell me about Romania," he says. "When God divided up the earth, he found that one place had everything. Mountains and rivers and forests and coal. And soil so rich, if you planted a fence post it grew into a tree. And peacocks roosting in every tree. That was Romania. Then God said, 'This is not fair.' So he made the stupidest people he could think of and put them there."

There are tears in Mihalik's eyes. When he wipes them with the back of his hand, some sawdust rubs off onto his beard. He looks grey and old.

"Remember when Nick first came to live with you?" Jared says. Mihalik rubs slow circles on the wood.

"You came to pick him up at kindergarten, and I was walking right next to him, and you asked me what's my name. And then you told me Nick's—Nikkolesh, something like that, you said."

"Nicolesçu," Mihalik says.

"And I told you that's too hard, that if he wanted to have friends he would have to be Nick."

"That night," Mihalik says, "before he went to bed, he brushed his teeth and combed his hair and put on his pajamas and slippers and came to say good night to me. 'Say good night to Nick,' he said."

"Nick brought me candy, once, in first grade," Jared said. "He said he was in bed already the night before, and then you came to get him and told him to put on some shorts and a T-shirt. You told him there was a special Romanian holiday called Pig Day, and that it just happened to be that day. You took him to the store to buy potato chips and candy and soda. And you and him ate that stuff, and sat up watching TV, and you said he didn't have to brush his teeth again, and he fell asleep on the couch and you slept there with him."

Jared is in Nick's room. He has a towel round his waist after his shower. He is getting dressed for the viewing. The suit Mihalik has bought is lying on the bed, with the shirt, socks and tie next to it. A pair of shoes stands toes together on the floor. Nick has a new outfit exactly like it, one size larger. Jared will see what he looks like in it when the family, which includes Jared and his mother, goes over an hour early for what Delia calls private time.

"Shit," Jared says. Mihalik has bought him everything except underwear. He will have to borrow some of Nick's.

In the closet beneath the boxers and sweat pants where Nick keeps his stuff that Mihalik is not supposed to see, Jared finds a packet of condoms and a computer disk with an adventure game he and Nick had copied from Larry Olsen only the week before. They have never even played it. It's called "Couch Fellatio."

Jared sits down on Nick's chair. He switches the computer on and boots the game. On the screen a man walks up to a girl sitting at a bar. "You have nice tits. Let's fuck," the synthesized computer voice says for him. The girl throws her drink at him. Then she strips off her top and licks the liquid off his face. The screen goes blank, and then it all happens from the beginning again.

"What the fuck is that?" Mihalik says from the door. He walks over and stands behind Jared.

Jared would normally have had to hide this from Mihalik, but now he doesn't care what he tells him. Nick is dead.

"A program we copied from Larry Olsen," he says.

"You little shithead," Mihalik says. "How can you play shit like this at a time like this."

Jared takes the disk out of the computer and puts it back in its paper sleeve. Something hard and splintery starts to push up under his heart. He walks over to the closet. At the shelf he lifts the clothes to hide the disk as usual, but then he feels Mihalik's eyes like ice cubes on his shoulder blades. He drops the disk in plain sight, then fumbles through the bundled clothes for the boxers he had forgotten to take the first time. The sting in his eyes blurs them all into the same dreary grey. When he finally pulls out a pair, Nick's *Playboys* topple over from behind the picture of Nick's mother and cascade past his ear onto the floor. When he grabs into the air above his head, he knocks down the cologne Nick had bought for the day when he was going to ask Becky Miller if she wanted to go to Hogi Yogi with them after school. It hits Nick's dumbbell on the way down and smashes with a tinkly glass sound.

"What the fuck," Mihalik says again.

Jared holds onto the shelf at the height of his chest. From behind him the cologne smell rises up like a promise so extravagant you know nothing will ever come of it. Jared knows he is going to cry and he doesn't try to stop. He hears his own voice, like a faraway siren.

He senses Mihalik coming up behind him even before he feels his hand on his shoulder. Mihalik's stomach feels warm against his back. Mihalik's arms are a clamp tightening around his body, as if they could keep things from falling apart. "Jared," Mihalik says, "tell me about Nick. What did he like? Did he ever say anything—?"

From the way Mihalik's fingers clench into his forearm, Jared knows what he wants to hear. But when he opens his mouth to say, "He loved you," no sound gets past the tight hurt in his throat. After he has coughed his voice back, he doesn't know anymore if Nick would have wanted him to say it. He thinks of the computer game in the closet. Nick liked hiding things from Mihalik. He thinks of the can of spray paint somewhere among the clothes, and of how cold it gets in your hand when you flick off the cap and push the button. Nick liked that too, but that's something Mihalik would never understand. He thinks of the packet of condoms on the top shelf. He remembers Fun Day, and the backseat in the bus where Nick sat with Becky Miller on the one side and he with Jennifer Tait on the other. Even if what Nick said about getting his hand all the way into Becky's panties were true, that was not enough for what Jared now could only guess Nick would one day have liked. Sounds that are not answers to Mihalik's question spill like vomit from his mouth.

Mihalik takes Jared by the shoulders and turns him so that they face each other. He, too, is shaking. When Jared looks up he sees Mihalik's top teeth biting down on his lower lip and his eyes squeezed tight to keep the sadness inside. Jared bites back his own gagging cries and reaches around Mihalik's waist and holds him. They rock to and fro together. After a while Mihalik pushes him away. "Time to go," he says.

At the funeral home Jared's mother stands at the door with Delia to greet them. While Delia talks to Mihalik, she walks in with Jared and holds his arm when he goes over to see Nick. Jared is glad she's there even though it is he who is keeping her from stumbling. She is very drunk. She looks magnificent, though. Her new red dress makes her hair look dyed.

Jared stands just close enough to see what Nick looks like. Nick's face is fatter than he remembers it, and bluish white. The suit makes him look dressed up for Halloween. He has nothing in his hands.

Mihalik comes over and stands on Jared's other side. He smells of Nick's cologne from cleaning up the spill. He reaches out his hand but he does not touch Nick. His fingers slide along the coffin's edge, tracing the scalloped lip that was so hard to sand.

Jared leans over and speaks close to Mihalik's ear. "Nick would like it," he says. "He would like it that you—that we—

made it." But what he thinks is that all this stuff about what Nick would like is just so they both can forget for a while that what Nick would actually like would be to be able to say for himself what it is that he would fucking like.

My Brother Can Tell

1. As large as a mouse's ear

On Mondays I visit my mother in the nursing home. I wash her hair with Clairol Silk and Silver because that is what she wanted when she could still say what she wanted. On this Monday when I get back home, I plant a quaking aspen in my front yard. On Tuesday morning only the hole is left. Someone has stolen my tree. I walk through my neighborhood, checking young trees for familiar patterns of venation. When I return, my son says, "Atilla the Hunter is playing with half a dead cat in the backyard."

"No," I correct. "Not half a dead cat. A half-dead cat." But then I start to wonder. I call my brother in Africa. My brother is sleeping and cannot be disturbed. I spell out this message to the head nurse of my brother's clinic: *Neighborhood crime rampant. Catch next flight home.*

"Hau," the head nurse says. "Lord Jesus be near you."

My brother is a medical missionary in Africa. Everyone knew early on he would become a doctor, because he won first place at the high school science fair for his cat skeleton. First he cooked a stray cat until the flesh fell from the bone. Overnight, however, our cat ate two cervical vertebrae drying on a towel, also causing severe damage to the lacrimal area of the skull. For another day another stray cat bubbled on the stove, filling the house with the tantalizing aroma of oxtail soup. During the assembly of the skeleton the spare parts came in handy, my brother said, when the pliers occasionally slipped from his normally steady grip and splintered some bones.

I am seven years older than my brother. On the day my mother was to go into labor with my brother, she dropped me off at school as usual. She did not know yet that would be the day. Neither, of course, did I. My brother was born on the day before Thanksgiving. We were doing Indians and Pilgrims in school at the time. Miss Turner showed pictures of Squanto, an Indian friend of the Pilgrims, who told them the best time to plant corn is "when the leaves of the white oak are as large as a mouse's ear." Squanto also showed the Pilgrims how to catch herrings from the brook and use them to fertilize the soil. In question time, when Miss Turner called on me, I said, "I have a new baby brother." Miss Turner, who had waved to my mother as she drove off, said, "Now, Trudy. Let's not allow our imaginations to run away with us." A few minutes later, while I was gluing the purple (for sorrow) corn onto my wampum apron, the secretary came into the room and whispered a message into Miss Turner's ear, and Miss Turner called me to her desk to tell me I had a new baby brother. My mother and Miss Turner, comparing schedules after the fact, interpreted my premature announcement as a clear case of childhood clairvoyance. Only I knew it was something I had made up to dispel the image of Pilgrims planting corn, of purple kernels dropped into furrows writhing with living fertilizer fresh from the brook.

In Africa my brother travels from one village to another, spreading the Word of God. If called aside and taken to a hut to issue a death certificate, my brother can tell exactly how many days the person has been dead: the millimeter length of the largest maggot plus two.

2. THE UNSPEAKABLE COLOR OF THINGS

Trudy, who has once been accused of lifting a setting from *National Geographic* to make a commonplace story seem exotic, confesses what she has told above is not altogether true. But she will try again. This time she is determined to keep it ordinary. She wants these people, as she tells them, to seem to you like a second cousin, a neighbor, an ex-roommate. She would like to keep the landscape local, would like to mention juniper and blue spruce, would like to reach no further than the bulbous scar on the trunk by her window where phloem and xylem are engulfing the anchor wire that was supposed to straighten the tree when it was still young. But she can see this is not going to be easy. Events are not so easily disconnected from their milieu, and information is stored everywhere, is carried from foreign parts into her back-yard, as when a flock of migratory birds settles on the parallel stretch of neighborhood power lines in the configuration of the first two bars of Strauss's *Parergon zur Symphonia domestica* that Wittgenstein adapted for one-handed piano and orchestra, not the Wittgenstein who maintained "philosophy is a battle against the bewitchment of our intelligence by means of language," but Wittgenstein the pianist who lost his right arm in World War I and acquired an amazing virtuosity with the left hand that enabled him to overcome difficulties formidable even to a two-handed pianist. Trudy, who cannot relate to playing the piano with one hand since she cannot play it with two, instead phones her brother long distance: Who held the hand of this man, she asks him, the left hand that could play so well, while he was eighty-four and dying in Manhasset, Long Island, in 1961, far from the hills alive with the music of his native Austria?

"Ma is not going to die," Trudy's brother says. Trudy can hear he is half asleep. "She's only seventy-nine. Her heart is strong."

"How do you know?" Trudy says. "You're not a doctor." (She really has a brother who is a doctor, but this is the other brother.) She waits for the yawning and stretching sounds to stop. "Gary likes the nail fetish you sent. He doesn't think you should have given it to Lewis, though. He wants to have it. He took it to school for show-and-tell. Someone broke off the penis, but Lewis glued it on again."

"Ow, ow," Trudy's brother says. He is awake by now. He is the brother who mumbles one nation under Snow White when he pledges allegiance to the flag, since he gave up God at approximately the same time Trudy did. He actually does not believe in pledging allegiance at all, but does not want to jeopardize his job in the CIA. "The teacher sent a note home," Trudy says. "She wants us to clear show-and-tell materials with her ahead of time in future."

"Remember when Mr. Greyling sent a note home?" Trudy's brother asks. "When we had lice? Do they still have lice?"

"Yes," Trudy says. "I'm a volunteer and I examine heads once a month. I send notes home."

"You'd think they wouldn't have lice anymore. Lice should be easier to eradicate than smallpox, for example. Take this hypothetical situation."

"They still have smallpox," Trudy says. "It has come back again." But then she says she has to go. This is not an excuse. One of Trudy's favorite things is talking through a gedankeneksperiment with her favorite brother, but she has heard a shout from Gary, her eight-year-old son, named for his Grandfather Bredenkamp, Trudy's father who died before Trudy became a mother. She hangs up on her brother, who won't stop talking, and runs off to look for her son.

She has to go no further than the deck outside the kitchen before she finds Gary. He is gesticulating wildly from the swaying top of the white ash level with their upstairs.

"There is half a dead cat in our yard," Gary shouts.

"No," Trudy corrects. "A half-dead cat."

But when she is face-to-face with her son, she sees from what Gary holds by its tail the error of assuming that what was wrong with what Gary said resided in the words. Not that we can blame her, for don't those of us who, like Trudy, are careful to say *African American* rather than *American black* rather than *negro* rather than *nigger* all subscribe to the idea that if we can change the words we can change the world? But what, Trudy wants to know, what do you insisters that the word determines the world rather than vice versa make of this?

Human DNA is built up of four bases, C (cytosine), G (guanine), A (adenine) and T (thymine). The first three bases have symbols corresponding to an existing musical notation. The transliteration of *mi* from thy*mi*ne allows the fourth base, T, to become E in the key of C and combine with the other three notes to sound the code of A minor. By adhering to these provisos and preserving proportionate note values to accommodate changes in meter, the first few bars of the melody of visual purple—the pigment required for the sensitization of the rod cells in the human eye to prevent night blindness—can be scored as follows:

"It has the flavor of an Irish jig," the one-handed Wittgenstein would say.

"Isn't this simply because if we think in signs, then we also expect and wish in signs?" the other Wittgenstein would respond.

Trudy agrees with both Wittgensteins, but what the second one would have said is more apropos to where her thoughts have rushed. Didn't she bring her husband Lewis, Gary's father, safely back from the Gulf War by replacing as it died each yellow rose in the bouquet that Lewis gave her on the day he left, so that the exact same bouquet was what Lewis saw on the credenza when he got back nine months later? Which reminds Trudy that she is a mother and that she has a son high up in a tree swinging half a cat by its tail.

"Give it to me, Baby," Trudy says. She takes Gary's find from him so he can make his way down unencumbered. "Mommy will get you a baggie and you can put it in the trash." When Trudy hunts in her kitchen for a baggie, she sees the picture she keeps on her fridge of Ted Bundy's mother, Louise Bundy, who had not wanted her son as a baby and now feels acutely the pain of his misdeeds as she hugs his empty Boy Scout uniform in her arms. Everyone knows what Ted Bundy used to do to cats. And Trudy knows that in this time of planned obsolescence, in this time of instant gratification, in this time of thousands of darling kittens facing euthanasia at animal shelters every day, that she has to make a stand for grief. That is why we find Trudy digging a grave in her front yard on her day off. She is digging it deep, so that there will be room for a quaking aspen above the shoe box with a drawing of a cat by Gary on its lid, a whole cat, the kind of cat one learns to draw in kindergarten, with two circles, two triangles, whiskers and a tail.

When she is done with planting, Trudy calls her other

brother, the medical missionary in Africa. She wants to tell him about the music in our genes. If there is one person in the world who should understand that words are related to real things, it is her brother the doctor. But Gerhard is not home. She was going to read him a paragraph she had torn from a magazine, so, instead, she dictates it to his head nurse: *David D. Reamer, molecular biologist, has analyzed one of Beethoven's hairs—from a keepsake lock of that wild mop included in his 1812 letter to his "Immortal Beloved"—and found encoded in the maestro's DNA the famous opening notes of his Fifth Symphony, T-T-T-C-C-C-C-C-C.*

Before Trudy can go on with this story, she has a confession to make. It is not her father who died while she was pregnant with Gary, but her mother. Trudy earlier picked her mother as the parent for this story, because there is too much to explain about her father before he starts sounding like a real person and not just a character she made up. In real life, however, it is Trudy's mother who died before Trudy became a mother. How inconsiderately she upstaged Trudy's pregnancy with her cirrhotic liver failure! In real life Trudy's father is the parent whose distant and unattended death Trudy now daily expects. Trudy's pledge to keep this story ordinary is what necessitated the substitution of mother for father. Trudy knows that her mother could be a mother anywhere in the world, could hide supplies of scotch, whiskey, or slivovitz with equal aplomb in toilet tanks, loo cisterns, or outhouses, but Trudy now knows that any parent will not do for what she wants to tell. She now wants to tell the story of her father, the particular father who ordered her brother who has now given up God and her brother who has now found Jesus to stretch the man who was their farm foreman, the black man, naked from the waist up, over an empty petrol drum by holding his arms (the brother who gave up God) and his legs (the brother who found Jesus), so that Trudy's father could sjambok him again and again while Trudy, who was excused from participation because she was a girl, watched from the top of a white stinkwood tree, a species that is rare to the point of extinction today because it's so highly valued for its cabinet wood, but which is in this story not because it is exotic but because *that was the tree.*

Gerhardus Joachim Hendrikus Bredenkamp was the name on two side-by-side graves in the graveyard through which Trudy passed every day on her way to primary school. Those were the names she had to trace on the headstones with her finger every day, no matter how urgently her brother shouted to hurry they'll miss the bus, because those were the graves of her father's two infant brothers who had his name briefly, in succession, before it was bestowed on Trudy's father. And everybody knew that every night after supper when Trudy's father sank into his chair by the radio he sighed, "I won't make old bones." (Trudy's father was not some crude hairyback farmer who divined water with a forked stick, but an educated man, an engineer, who had a black box that measured drops in the electrical resistance of under- ground formations, and who had found gushing water veins on three neighboring farms. It was not his water-detecting activities that made him tired, though, but having to help Trudy and her brother with their homework after a hard day supervising his laborers, because Trudy's mother had headaches and could not help with anything, but had to lie in a dark room before and after supper.)

Next to the baby graves, on the side nearest the bus stop, was a double plot with Trudy's Grandfather Bredenkamp on the one side, and a space on the other side, the headstone all filled in and ready for Grandmother Bredenkamp except for the date of death, because Grandmother Bredenkamp was then still in the back bedroom with the drawn curtains, trying to die. Every afternoon after school Trudy and her brother were required to say good day to Grandma Bredenkamp, and on the days when Grandma noticed them she directed them to the drawer by her bedside that smelled of licorice allsorts (but it was actually the Dutch Drops for her nerves) to help themselves to half a crown each from her stash of Jubilee coins. Trudy's brother sometimes took an extra coin, but Trudy never did, except once, to reward herself for hearing out a confidence Grandma Bredenkamp whispered with rotten breath in her ear: that the coins were to go to Old Hester, the Xhosa servant who washed Ouma Bredenkamp's diapers and sheets, not so much as a reward for what she was doing for Ouma Bredenkamp right then, because that was expected of a servant, but for what she did for Trudy's father when he was an infant and Ouma Bredenkamp was so sick her milk dried up.

After Ouma Bredenkamp had died, as soon as the undertakers had taken her away, Old Hester cleaned out her room and gave the coins to Trudy and her brother to share, asking if she could keep for herself two medallions, a gilt one with Prime Minister Verwoerd on it, and a black enamel one in the shape of an open book with Die Wonder van Afrikaans, *The Miracle of Afrikaans, 1875–1955*, printed across the pages. Trudy could see both of these medallions glittering on Old Hester's head cloth as her head bobbed in a hymn on the servants' side of the grave during the funeral. Years later, when Trudy had become a mother herself and was watching with bursting love the nod of her son's head at her breast, she remembered Old Hester. When her father, who could then still talk, came to see his grandson, she asked him about her.

"She's been dead for many a year," Trudy's father said. "What made you think of her?"

When Trudy told him, he denied everything, even though by then J. A. Heese had published evidence proving that literally hundreds of the most prominent Afrikaans families have nonwhite blood in their veins, so that having once sucked at a black breast should not have jeopardized Trudy's father's position in the National Party. Trudy was taken unawares by her father's denial, because it was not like her father to care about what other people thought anyway, because when he was still on the farm he wore white shirts with his khaki shorts, and not khaki shirts like the other farmers, a sartorial statement about which several farmers' wives berated Trudy's mother, saying that it looked as if Trudy's father thought he was above their husbands because of his education, but her father never relented. On Sundays he wore a black suit and a white shirt like the other church deacons, and as soon as he got home he took off the suit and put on khaki shorts, but he kept on his black shoes and socks, except for the Sunday when they found their tractor driven into a donga by the side of the road on their way home from church when he did not stop even to take off his jacket before hauling the foreman out of his shack and over the petrol drum, so that with the first crack of the sjambok a rip appeared over her father's shoulderblade in the black suit material that breathed gulps of blue silk lining with every subsequent lift of his arm, a blue the same sky blue as the blue caught in the reflection of Trudy's mother's bedroom window, from where Trudy could feel her mother's gaze penetrating her white church dress and focusing on her heart pulsing wetly between her legs as she clasped them around the stinkwood trunk.

A few more things have to be set straight at this point. Trudy's brother who gave up God is not in the CIA, but that is how she had to tell it in order to make the story local. In real life this brother is a computer communications expert who lives in Johannesburg, and the anecdote about Snow White is actually advice this brother gave to Trudy for when she imminently has to pledge allegiance to the American flag, because Trudy is about to become a citizen of the United States of America, and she would rather just be a citizen of the world.

It is true that both Trudy and her one brother gave up God at about the same time, and that the other brother found Jesus— he tells it the other way round, insisting it is Jesus who found him—but it is not true that he is a medical missionary in Africa. He is just a doctor who happens to have been born in South Africa and who gives his patients the Good News with their kwashiorkor shots and their soy meal rations. Trudy envies him for the opportunity to make good the sins of our fathers generally, and in particular the opportunity that presented itself in the shape of the farm foreman whose legs he'd held when he was five years old, and who showed up out of the blue at his free Saturday clinic. When Trudy's doctor-brother prostrated himself before the old man and held onto his legs and asked his forgiveness in the name of Jesus, the old man pulled out of his grasp with surprising vitality and went to the end of another doctor's queue, leaving Trudy's doctor-brother stricken with the insight that the foreman, who was a young and strapping man at the time of the punishment, could not possibly have been held down by a five-year-old boy (the legs) and an eleven-year-old boy (the arms) unless he had been to some extent cooperative.

Trudy is a year older than her computer-expert brother, Nick, named out of sequence for their mother's father, because at the time of his birth it seemed Trudy's parents were going to have this one son only, since Trudy's mother almost died in childbirth and one could not imagine she would be capable of producing another son so that her family's name would be perpetuated according to the customary sequence: a first son is named for his father's father, and a second son for his mother's father. As it happened, Trudy's mother did unexpectedly become expectant again when Trudy was in first grade, giving birth during second grade to the brother who would one day find Jesus, and whom she then named Gerhardus after his paternal grandfather, and incidentally after his father as well.

On the day when Gerhard was to be born, Nick and Trudy caught the green school bus as usual, and only when they were way on the other side of the kaffirs' shacks did Trudy realize she had forgotten the kaffir corn for the maphoto apron they were making in social studies with Mister Greyling. Once before when Trudy had forgotten something—her *Sus en Daan* reader— Mister Greyling had called her to his table and stuck his hand under her bottle green school dress and through the leg elastic of her bottle green school panties and pinched her bottom so she would never, never again forget anything at home.

Although Trudy has since given up God, she still has no other word than "vision" for what spared her Mister Greyling's corrective hand in her panties on that day. At the very moment when Mister Greyling started calling up everyone who had forgotten their kaffir corn or rice or yellow mealies, Trudy knew with the utmost certainty that she had a new baby brother.

"We have a new baby," Trudy said when Mister Greyling asked why she had forgotten the kaffir corn. Mister Greyling, who imparted punishment for lying—which was worse than forgetting—in the storeroom off the classroom, took Trudy by the hand and led her to the principal's office to call Trudy's home. Their maid, Serafina, answered and said the missus could not come to the phone because she had gone to the maternity home. This surprised everyone since nobody had known about the pregnancy, because Trudy's mother had by then taken Ouma Bredenkamp's place in the back bedroom and hadn't been leaving the house much. When all the evidence had been pieced together, it transpired that Trudy had made her announcement at the exact same moment when Dr. von Pletzen had said, "It's a boy."

Mister Greyling, who knew about these things, told Trudy's father this was a clear case of childhood clairvoyance. The only person who knew Trudy had made it up was her brother Nick, but she knew he wouldn't tell since he was in Mister Greyling's class too—the second and third grade shared a teacher—and he admired Trudy's inventiveness and tried the same trick himself the next time it became necessary to avoid Mister Greyling's corrective hand, only it did not work again since Trudy's mother had no more children after Gerhardus.

One last thing. The war that Trudy brought her husband Lewis back from by replacing as it died each flower in the bouquet he gave her on the day he left was nothing as exotic as the Gulf War, since it happened right there on their own country's border and as Shabbir Banoobhai says so stunningly in his poem "the border," the border / is as far / as the black man / who walks alongside you. In fact, it wasn't even a war at all, although thousands of people got killed in it, and Lewis himself killed two of them that he knows of. Lewis doesn't think he survived because Trudy kept the flowers alive. He knows he is lucky.

"Lewis is lucky," Trudy says in a different context, because she is jealous that Lewis's name is eminently pronounceable to Americans. Trudy's name is not really Trudy, but that is what she goes by since the Americans cannot say Truia. Some of her good friends want to, but they forget how to in between appellations, so Trudy has to coach them time and time again on the pronunciation of the Afrikaans triphthong *uia:* Shape your mouth into an *o* and then say *a.* Follow with an *ah!*

Now the phone rings and when Trudy says, "This is Trudy," there is someone on the other end who actually calls her Truia. Miss Truia, to be exact. It is Homeboy Maletsu, her brother the doctor's head nurse.

"How are you, Homeboy?" Trudy asks.

"We all in good health this side, praise the Lord."

"How are the grandchildren?"

"Beauty and Ethel are getting big now. They be starting school in the new year. The doctor gave the money for their uniforms. I gave your message to the doctor."

"Where is my brother, Homeboy? Let me speak to him."

"He was called out to the country, Miss Truia. He looked up a piece in a book for you. He said I must read it to you."

"Okay, Homeboy," Trudy says. "I'm listening."

This is what Homeboy reads haltingly: *The most powerful element in the first movement of Beethoven's third symphony* (Eroica) *is undoubtedly the two-bar unit, two great E-flat major chords, which rivet our attention and propel the action. When once asked what his symphony "meant," the maestro walked over to the piano and played the first eight notes of his theme that simply outline the key of E-flat. It was all the answer he gave.*

"Is that the whole message, Homeboy?" Trudy asks. She has

been hoping for news of her father. He is being cared for in Gerhard's home. "Didn't he say anything about my father?"

"I can tell you about the old master," Homeboy says. "He is as good as can be expected, praise the Lord. His spirit is still strong. Yesterday he did not want to let me wash him. He kicked and he knocked the water on the floor. So Beauty and Ethel helped me. The one held the hands and the other one the feet. The old master kept still then. How are you, Miss Truia? When are you coming home?"

"This is our home now, Homeboy," Trudy says. "We have bought a flag set for the Fourth of July. I have planted a tree. Do you know who Ray Charles is, Homeboy?"

"Ray Charles," Homeboy says. "No Ma'am. But you tell me, I'll write his number down."

"Ray Charles is a black singer, Homeboy. He is very famous. He is blind. Gerhard likes his music. Tell Gerhard I said Ray Charles said if he had to choose between blindness and his music, he would not want to lose his musical ability just to be able to see."

"Our blacks have that trouble here too, Ma'am," Homeboy says. "Vitamin A deficiency, glaucoma, papilledema, retrobulbar neuritis."

Trudy puts the phone down. She goes outside to look at her quaking aspen. She sees someone has stolen her tree. Only the hole is left. As she walks about the neighborhood checking young trees for familiar patterns of venation, she longs for her doctor-brother, the brother who goes out to far-flung villages to offer

Christian burials and official death certificates. This is the brother whom Trudy brought back to life when she was seven years old and when he was a newborn baby, on his first day home from the maternity hospital, but she has never told him this. Nobody in the world knows about this except maybe Trudy's father.

Trudy's mother was already asleep in the back bedroom. Trudy and her brother Nick watched while her father gave the baby its bottle. When the baby was done drinking, Trudy's father laid it down on the other half of his big bed. He himself fell asleep with his clothes on, on top of the covers. Trudy and Nick tiptoed to their own room and put themselves to bed. Sometime during the night Trudy was awakened by a wail that echoed in the hollows of her bones. The moonlight felt cold on her skin as she made her way to her father's room. Trudy's father slept while the baby beat the air with its fists. At the moment when Trudy reached for the baby it stopped crying and was still. Trudy had never seen a baby that still. Her finger hardly knew how to make the letters when she traced the baby's name on its chest. Gerhardus Joachim Hendrikus Bredenkamp. Without the guiding grooves of the gravestone, she must have missed some of the letters, for it did not help. The only breathing Trudy could hear was that of her father. She climbed onto the bed and seated herself cross-legged next to the baby, with her back against the wall. She pulled her pajama top off over her head and dropped it onto the floor. Her chest was the unspeakable color of things that live in dark places. Her nipples poked through the blue-white skin like the heads of maggots. Trudy picked up the baby and pushed its mouth over her nipple, and felt the surprising pain when her brother came to life and sucked. For a long time Trudy listened to the miracle of milk squirting from her flat breasts into her brother's mouth, until she could no longer distinguish that liquid sound from the sound of her father's weeping.

Blessings on the Sheep Dog

Speedy wants to get some terminology agreed upon before we get any further into this. Speedy does not speak well, so he does not want to backtrack, explain, go over the same ground more than once. He knows listening to him is a strain, so he is trying to get to the point. What I learn first is that a defective gene makes his skull outgrow the muscles of his face, squeezes his eyes into a permanent bulge, and stretches his vocal cords so that a high-pitched whine is what his tongue and taut-skinned lips are forever struggling to modulate. That understood, he wants to start at the beginning, which would mean starting with Samantha and O'Neill, and that is where he first runs into the extreme paucity of the English language when it comes to nomenclature for describing relationships. For the purposes of telling, Speedy at first thinks "Sam's husband O'Neill" will do for what O'Neill had been of Samantha's. But then Speedy's daughter Alexandra, over whose bath he is presiding from a stool by the side, juts a soapy elbow at an angle which places her on the trajectory to his heart. His *daughter* Alexandra?

The label for what Alexandra is to Speedy turns inside out and brims with newness like the ancient face of a newborn.

"Eighty-six times!" Alexandra says.

Speedy is studying a photograph before reading the letter that has been folded around it. He holds it out so I can see. Then he turns the picture toward Alexandra. "Eighty-six times," he says, reading from the back. "That's what Sam says." For the truth of the words the little girl depends on him, because she does not yet know how to read cursive. Today's mail is the latest from Samantha, Alexandra's *blank blank* (while Speedy rethinks relationship labels). "The Dingle Burn. It curves and curves like this." Speedy makes a sine wave above the bathwater, using Alexandra's body as the x-axis. "So if she keeps going in the same direction like this," tracing Alex's leg in the steam, "she crosses it again and again. In a river that is called meandering. Now wash your feet."

Since Alexandra's fifth birthday Speedy has thought it prudent to assist merely verbally in her bath. As with everything that concerns Alexandra, Speedy wants to do things right. "Left knee, vulva, right knee, stomach." Then he reads out loud from the letter.

"Those New Zealand rivers," Alexandra says over his laboring voice. "What is the autumn muster, Daddy?"

I know I'm here only to observe, but I almost say it: Oh, the furious rivers, the creaking glaciers, the tussocky basins of New Zealand's high country!

It is Speedy who speaks. "It's when Sam gets up at four in the morning," he says, "and has a breakfast of mutton chops and tea and goes into the mountains with some men and dogs to round up the sheep."

"I want some Choculas when I'm done," Alex says. "You said."

"Then you have to brush your teeth again. Not many people know this." He is on the second page. Where Samantha has underlined his voice drops into a purposeful alto. "'The hunt-away dogs of the New Zealand High Country were originally taken there from the English-Scotland border. The farmers say that the border collies *made this country*. On the shore of Lake Tekapo there is a statue of a collie, with a plaque in Gaelic: *Beannachdan air na Cu Caorach—Blessings on the Sheep Dog.*'" While Alexandra steps shivery onto the floor, he skims through to the bottom line of Sam's x-ed kisses. His hands through terry rub warmth into her back as he tells the rest of the news short and sweet: "On cold nights during the muster, Sam says, she lets some of her favorite dogs sleep on top of her, on top of her sleeping bag. A very cold night is known as a three-dog night."

"Three dog night," our Alex sings to the tune of "Three Blind Mice." She is belting it out. "Three dog night. / See how they run, / See how they run."

"What color eyes did you pick for baby?" Alexandra wants to know. It is bedtime, and they are playing Scrabble. To even out the odds between them, they have a rule: Alexandra plays with seven tiles, and Speedy with four.

"You don't really pick," Speedy says. "You have to wait and see how it comes out. Say the donor has blue eyes. The surrogate's eyes are grey. So we're looking at a light color, anyway. Like yours."

"We're not looking at a color," Alexandra says. "The eyes aren't here yet. We're looking at letters." Triumphantly she turns her tiles toward him.

"PENNIS," Speedy reads. If O'Neill had been here, Speedy would tell me after Alex has been tucked in, he would have reached to take one of the N's out. As for Speedy, he wants to take the whole word away. But he censors himself. If Alexandra brings it up, the book says, no topic is too early for discussion.

"Pennies," Alexandra says, "like the ones that rained on the good daughter in Mother Holly."

"From heaven," Speedy says. "An eight-point word! Where did I get you from?" The last is just one of those things one says when love expands with unbearable pressure under one's breastbone, because in reality Speedy knows exactly where Alexandra came from.

So does Alexandra. "From Sam's uterus," she says. "Double word score. What's eight and eight?"

This is what Speedy tells me later and will eventually tell Alexandra over years of bath and bed times. Sam and O'Neill, and his college friend Speedy Harrison ("That's you, Daddy!" Alex will say, calling him on it as usual when he tries to get away with making himself a character in one of his stories) rented a lot where they made paint in a shed that shivered with the hum of the agitators they had bought with the lump sum Sam got when she sued a previous employer for failing to prevent distribution of a batch of paint in which the severed and crushed finger of her left hand, including her grandmother's birthstone ring, had been accidentally incorporated. Until the county could who knows when afford to repaint the library, Sam told the judge, the glitter of ground amethyst off its exterior caused her mental anguish every time she drove down Main Street.

In truth the judge did not buy this story, but since he started sleeping with her as soon as the case was over, he must have looked on his award as a kind of preemptive palimony. As for the missing finger, her ring finger—once the pain was over, Sam regarded it fondly as a sign that God did not want her to get married. But when she soon afterwards again came face-to-face with mental anguish, she found no succor in the absence for which, uncannily, a batch of paint was once again the visible sign.

As Sam would later tell Speedy, and as Speedy is now telling me, she knew that something was wrong when Speedy instead of O'Neill walked in on her one Friday evening while she was hunched over some papers at the dining room table. Sam applying herself was so unusual a sight, that Speedy was later able to recall that she was frowningly counting days with the help of a calendar and her nine fingers.

"O'Neill . . . is . . . dead," Speedy said. He had picked his words for their simplicity, since his speech is frequently misunderstood even under normal circumstances. Since Sam nevertheless appeared uncomprehending, he found himself relating what the cops had told him: that O'Neill was going far too fast and had an open beer in the cab when he drove his truck through the highway barrier at the cloverleaf interchange; that it happened en route to the airport where he was heading with the forty gallons of that vomit-yellow paint that she had helped him to shade less than two hours before; that the road had to be closed because of cars slip-sliding in the paint.

O'Neill's body, which Sam immediately went to see with Speedy, looked unremarkably the same as usual. The usualness at least is what Speedy likes to foreground when he tells the story to Alexandra. To himself he admits, however, that it was most unusual to be in a semipublic place with both Sam and her naked lover. And the next part Speedy never mentions to Alexandra, although to this day the memory of Sam's assault on O'Neill is his most vivid one, in retrospect made absolutely forgivable by her look of bafflement, as if there was a complete lack of connection between her fists hammering on O'Neill's chest and his lips burbling a foamy pink "B-b-b" with each blow.

Speedy had restrained her with a strong-armed grip. Sam later told him she believed that had been his first opportunity ever to clasp the whole length of a woman against his body. (She was wrong.) Speedy further inferred that his grip must have made some kind of impression on her, because it was for more of the same that she returned again and again during the following days.

Now there's something else Speedy wants to explain. His initial impulse to refer to O'Neill as Sam's "husband" has nothing to do with coyness, since he knows that worse things are going to come out than that Sam and O'Neill were not married. Nor is it out of any impulse to protect Sam from what might be concluded from her attitude toward relationships, because Speedy realized long ago that Sam does not need any protection, long before she left him Alexandra three days old and a stack of children's books in which all the heroes were heroines. Sam just does not care about labels. "Why must O'Neill be my something?" Sam would say. "O'Neill is O'Neill and I am me." No, Speedy's groping for a term that describes O'Neill in terms of what he was of Sam's says something about the basic organization of the human being, for who do *you* know (I'm assuming you don't know Sam) who does not define him- or herself as somebody's something?

Alexandra calls from her room, and Speedy goes to her prepared with a glass of water. It is not water she wants. She has something on her mind. "I am disappointed in Sam," she says. "I have always, always wanted a koala. I don't want a tuatara." She throws the toy across the room.

Speedy has to agree. Sam did write and promise a koala, but that was when she was still heading for Australia. On the way she met a rancher going home to his station in the New Zealand high country. Speedy forgives her, even for the broken promise. For the gift of Alexandra he has forgiven and will forgive Sam everything. He offers peace. "A tuatara is even more special than a koala." He picks up the toy and puts it on the shelf. "Your tuatara is like a dinosaur that just didn't become extinct. And it even has a third eye on its forehead."

"Real ones," Alexandra says. "This old one is plastic. It has only two eyes. And it's hard. I like soft." And she's not done. "I'm disappointed in you too, Daddy. I told you banana. I told you the apricot makes my mouth like I want to give someone a kiss. But today in my lunch—apricot again."

Speedy has no defense. He lingers quietly in the doorway for a while. Banana, banana, banana, he mouths, committing Alexandra's desire to memory.

Although Speedy and O'Neill had not lived together since they shared a room in college, they were together often enough so that people who ran into Speedy cradling a drum of paint asked, "Where's that O'Neill today?" Speedy had been there, in fact, when Sam and O'Neill fell in love, although they, like all lovers, were oblivious to anything but each other. Aside from the red hairs in O'Neill's beard, Speedy thinks, it was the fact that he took Sam's mind seriously that did it. *Taking someone's mind seriously* was the kindest spin anyone could put on O'Neill's pedantic way of explaining things, and that was what Sam chose to believe. Speedy was used to O'Neill, and only noticed his sententiousness because he looked at everything those days to see what it might seem like through Sam's eyes.

For example. At the "Festival of Oldies" O'Neill, Sam, and Speedy were watching *Mr. Smith Goes to Washington.* In the darkened theatre Sam remarked that the light beam from the projector appeared blue, while the light on the screen was white. O'Neill pontificated: This same scattering of the blue components of white light by particles in the atmosphere is what makes the sky blue. Speedy's dark-adapted eyes saw Sam's hand reach between O'Neill's legs and fiddle around until O'Neill's moaning made someone behind them say, "Shut the fuck up."

"*Shut the fuck up,*" O'Neill repeated pensively. Turning to face his accuser, he embarked on another lecture. "Inserting words into a compound term. *What place soever* is the example you'll find in most dictionaries. Informally known as a kangaroo word. The technical term, I believe, is tmesis."

For reasons of his own, Speedy heard *tumescence.* Out of habit Speedy thought not of Sam or O'Neill, as you may be imagining, but of the only real "spouse" in this story: O'Neill's wife, Rebecca, the girl whose sensible habits and freckled breasts had determined the wholesome notion of sex that had at that time governed Speedy's imagination. That day in the theatre, as the person behind them said, "Moron," and moved to a seat further back, and as O'Neill launched into the terms applicable to specific IQ ranges, it struck Speedy that O'Neill had never gotten around to divorcing Rebecca.

Words never failed O'Neill. By contrast, as I have experienced by now, talk sometimes comes from Speedy's mouth detached from meaning. Which he knows. So that when I'm still on the ex of "Excuse me?" he is already rephrasing, saying it again. Moreover, Speedy cannot smile. No matter how hilarious the joke, Speedy's face remains expressionless while he tries to make up for his shortcoming by a knee-slapping show of hilarity. Despite his inadequacies from the neck up, however, Speedy with his strong arms and his monkey wrench is the person you would want around when a puddle appears on the floor around your toilet bowl on the morning after your lover has died.

When Sam was brought to a halt in front of the toilet that morning, she did not have to phone Speedy at his place on the rented lot, but only had to shout out the door to the adjacent room where he was asleep in O'Neill's chair. Like many of us Sam probably thinks of emotions in Aristotelian pairs: grief/joy, love/hate, fear/trust. Therefore (and this is Speedy's theory to explain why Sam, as if for the first time, suddenly noticed him) she must have been startled when he took one look at the seeping toilet and started to cry; when it became clear to her that, even though he could not smile, Speedy could weep like anyone else.

At Speedy's place, where they had gone to use the toilet, Sam looked about as if she was noticing other things about Speedy for the first time. His hobby: he took X-rays of vegetables and flowers, exposing the fractal architecture of fruiting bodies, the fragile structures of pistils and stamens.

"Color gets in the way," Speedy said.

"That reminds me," Sam said. "That was the paint guy on the phone this morning. He's after his forty gallons."

"I hope you wrote the pigments down," Speedy said.

"They're in my head," Sam said.

And they were, but so were many other things. Some of them propelled her screaming from her bed into Speedy's during the night that followed a day during which, for some moments, they had been able to forget that O'Neill was dead while reproducing the exact shade of the peculiar pinkish yellow paint. That night— what with one form of comfort leading to another—Sam and Speedy made love for the first time. They made love some subsequent times between the delivery of the paint order first thing the next morning and O'Neill's funeral later the same day.

Speedy ascribes the blissful times that followed to Sam's discovery that being listened to constituted a pleasant change from being talked at, and to his own habituation to the delicate structures of the female body, to the most amazing dimples on Sam's shoulders which made it seem as if she were smiling from the inside out as a result of his increasingly skillful manipulations.

A result of this bliss was that Speedy revised his earlier construction of the love/sex pair of concepts. Up till this time love and sex had appeared to Speedy to have little to do with each other. As a child he had associated conjugal love with the imprint of his mother's fingernails on his father's arm on the occasion at the doctor's office when the fate of his face was being given a name. He then had neither the knowledge nor the imagination to disengage his parents' subsequent daily assignations of genetic blame to each other from the thrashings that came from their bedroom on Sunday nights, and which he interpreted as punitive rather than as orgasmic. Romantic love to Speedy had meant O'Neill. Sex, on the other hand, had consisted of fantasies not excluding O'Neill, but also including whoever it was O'Neill's more practical experience involved at the time. Speedy himself was not totally lacking in practical experience, but his practice involved mostly himself, with the exception of two or three memorable occasions predicated upon darkness and money, in which he was relieved of the necessity of a solo performance. For Speedy the unexpected coincidence of love and sex in his energetic feats with Sam was something to be celebrated with the appreciation of a man who knew what he did not deserve.

Speedy wants to gloss over the three months following O'Neill's death, at the end of which the physical phase of his and Sam's intimacies ended, and move on to what he considers to be the events that showed their relationship in a truer light. I inform Speedy that Michel Foucault, philosopher and historian, believes that "it is sex itself which hides the most secret parts of the individual: the structure of his fantasies, the roots of his ego, the forms of his relationship to reality." So we will have to ask for Speedy's cooperation awhile longer. Speedy refuses. Speaking as an example of a monstrous miscarriage of biological justice, Speedy says, he will . . . not . . . indulge . . . any . . . morbid . . . curiosity. He will not barter his cooperation for our sympathetic understanding of his condition. But he will say something about Sam: Sam invited every woman O'Neill had ever dated and/or slept with to his funeral, including the wife who was then his widow.

Speedy thinks that except for the absence of sex—or maybe even because of it—"husband and wife" very closely describes the tranquil domesticity of his and Sam's days during the last trimester of her pregnancy. But then, what does Speedy know about marriage, or even about living with a woman? The extent of Speedy's ignorance struck him one day, three months after O'Neill's death, when certain almost-forgotten facts from tenth grade biology occurred to him while he watched Sam's cavorting at the tip of his finger.

"Aren't . . . you . . . supposed . . . to get . . . your period . . . some . . . time?" Speedy asked.

"I'm pregnant," Sam said.

It is six years now since Sam made her announcement. On the spiraling ramp of the cloverleaf interchange those who know where to look can still find pinkish yellow splotches of paint, faded now. Speedy is still making paint. The shed has recently made way for a new building, efficient but more modest than initially planned, since Speedy decided to skim ten thousand dollars off the loan to pay a surrogate for another baby. Speedy had hoped for a smaller gap between Alexandra and the baby, but for some reason or another it took the surrogate eighteen months and eleven procedures at the medical center to get pregnant, with Speedy agonizing all over again about which donor to pick every time.

Eighteen months and eleven procedures later it is clear to me what's in it for Speedy, but every day it's harder for the surrogate. Ten thousand dollars now seems much less to her than eighteen months ago, since she has already run up that much in student loans. Moreover, she did not bargain on being pregnant during her final year in graduate school. In the beginning her abortive attempts to conceive were irritating, an embarrassing failure of bodily functions, a loss of face since she had told Speedy she got pregnant if I—Yes, I said I. And I'll let it stand, I suppose—as much as French-kissed a man. But lately it was the fear that I might conceive that has haunted me more, that once I will have delivered there would be no more dates at the clinic, no soothing hand stroking mine when I have to lie with my legs in the stirrups for an hour afterwards. In front of Speedy I make light of my failure. Must be because there's no kissing in French or any other language at the medical center, I told him the last time he took me in.

Speedy's expression reached new levels of vacuity. But I found out soon enough that he had seen right through me. The moment I told him that this time it had taken, that I had tested positive, he asked me to come over. He wanted to tell me what had happened before, so I would clearly understand that this time he is determined to pay in hard currency only.

Once Alexandra has settled down, he makes no bones about it. He has chosen me rather than an American, he says, precisely because my student visa will run out in a year and I will have to return to South Africa. He has banned the word "mother" from his vocabulary, he says.

"Words have a way of creeping back," I say.

"Sign this," Speedy says.

My pen is in my hand. Very few people know this, and I think O'Neill would have been one of them. There is a sentence in

Afrikaans which has exactly the same words as a sentence in English. This sentence means exactly the same thing in both languages. Only the pronunciation is different. *My pen is in my hand.* Exactly the same thing. Until you start fucking with the words. *My hen is in my pand.* Now, in Afrikaans that might be construed to mean that my hen is part of my dowry. In English it sucks. *My penis in my hand.* Most people think that semen donors ejaculate into a bottle. They don't. They ejaculate into a condom. The surrogate is spared all this mess and gets the ejaculate through a syringe from someone wearing rubber gloves. *Pennis from heaven.*

I haven't signed yet, so Speedy keeps talking. What he tells me strengthens my belief in the open destiny of events not yet lived through.

After Sam's announcement, he confirmed her pregnancy with a home testing kit. He then arranged for an abortion as soon as possible. Sam did not fuss. She'd had abortions before. And that is where the story would have ended, if it hadn't been for Speedy wanting to do things right. He was going to hold Sam's hand. He got her into it, he was going to be there for her.

They checked in at the clinic. "Last period?" the nurse asked. "Estimated age of fetus?"

Speedy was stunned as he listened to Sam's answers. Her pregnancy predated her and his couplings by several weeks. Leaning with an elbow on the reception desk, he recalled dates crossed off on the kitchen calendar and the positions of Sam's calculating fingers on the night of O'Neill's death.

"This is O'Neill's baby," he said.

Sam said, "Of course it's O'Neill's baby. But it doesn't matter whose baby it is. I'm not having it anyway."

Speedy dragged Sam from the counter and immediately and terrifyingly exposed her to his expressionless fury. "You were going to kill O'Neill's baby," he said again and again, unbelievingly. Sam took less time to say, "Fine, okay, I'll have it then," than it takes her to choose between blue cheese and ranch. Beached on the couch from that day on, she had plenty of time to exact payment. Speedy paid with the abandon of someone who had won the lottery. No matter how many times per day Sam said, "I don't like X," Speedy took it away and tried again. Body and soul he nourished her. She disdained with equal loathing the latest best-seller or her hitherto favorite movie. She rejected with great impartiality chocolates from Switzerland and stir-fried cruciform veggies bursting with the entire alphabet of vitamins. "It just gets in my mouth," Sam said.

Speedy was patient. He soothed. He coaxed. He found cottage cheese with a curd size acceptable to Sam. Speedy, as you can see, is the only one in this story who can truly be called a *wife*.

As for Alexandra, she knows most of this. When she calls Speedy to her room again, she has a different question.

"What will the baby be of me, Daddy?" she asks.

Speedy considers hyphens and exes and possessives, and cops out. "If it's a girl it will be your sister, and if it's a boy it will be your brother."

Alexandra seems satisfied. She is very sleepy now. She sucks on the ribbon from her nightdress, and when she speaks again she mumbles as inaudibly as Speedy usually does. It sounds as if she's asking who is going to be the baby's Sam, but if that *is* what she's asking, Speedy is not answering. No words come out of his mouth as the softness of Alexandra's cheek passes beneath the stretched skin of his lips.

Speedy comes back and sits down in the rocker across from where I am feet up on the couch. He is looking at me. Under his gaze I feel my belly expand, feel the tautening of my skin into a silver-white meander of stretch marks. But Speedy is the kind of person who will want to look deeper than the surface. Maybe he is thinking right now how to achieve that, how to deliver the exact pulse and dosage of flash X-ray that would reveal the delicate fetal bones without obscuration by the more dense and mature surrounding skeleton. Or maybe he is thinking what would happen if he were to get up, and come over, and ask (even though speech is never easy) if he might feel beneath the skin for what will soon be his.

We'll Get to Now Later

STAN AND CECILIA

After six, seven years as an immigrant Stan retained the tendency of non-native English speakers to drop words such as *hirsute* into casual conversation. He also, I remembered, had a preference for smoothly ironed underwear. Other than that, he could probably pass tolerably well for an American. That is, until the incident that caused his wife to send him packing. For on this occasion, the person he chose to confide in was two continents and nine time zones away. He called me, oblivious of the time difference, when most people here were asleep. He did not identify himself, but went straight at it: *he stormed into the house bearing the front door*, as the Afrikaans expression has it.

"Cecilia asked me to leave," he said. His voice came across the distance tinged with indignation. I knew it was him right away.

"In fact," he continued, "she threw me out. She did not even let me pick up my electric razor."

In my sleep-drugged state, the image of Stan unshaven and

distraught led to thoughts of a kind I would not have entertained had I been fully awake. By the time he had gone on to describe the circumstances that had led to his wife's outrage, however, I had pulled myself together. My thoughts had turned to Cecilia. And the children. "How are the boys handling it?" I asked.

"They haven't really noticed. It's only been a few hours. She's let me speak to them on the phone. I told them I was going to be away on a business trip for a few days. I hope it will have blown over by then."

In anyone other than Stan, the belief that a calamity of this order would soon dissipate would have surprised me. The Stan I know, however, is not given to dwelling on the past. He is quick to let bygones be bygones, and expects no less from those around him. What I have loved most about him through the years—and I am not alone, but I may have been the first—was just this: his ability to plunge into each moment as if no time preceded it and no consequences would flow from it. Which used to make for strange bedfellows, inclined as I am to live my life in the afterglow of a single epiphany. But that is my story. Now it's time for Stan's.

Some weeks after his wife Cecilia had told him to leave, Stan stood on the deck of his new bachelor's quarters in Salt Lake City, Utah, grilling sausages for himself and his boys. He was marveling at how rooted in the present he was, for he was thinking *Brown bird dive-bombing grill,* rather than one of a class of more nostalgic thoughts, like, *In the Magalakweno District it is possible to tell whether it will rain from the whiteness of the egrets.*

When he was fifteen and in love for the first time—this was twenty-five years ago—there came a morning three months into the infatuation when he realized he had not yet that day thought of his love, Henrietta, even though he'd already had a shit and a shower. She occupied a room in the girls' hostel across the street from the boys' hostel where he had been, that moment, arrested mid-shave. For her he had switched the light of his room on and off in rapid succession at eleven P.M. the night before. Then he waited for her answering flicker as he had done for the preceding three months, after which he had masturbated and fallen into a dreamless sleep. That morning he woke with all memory of Henrietta temporarily erased. But the burden of being in love returned as soon as the peculiar weightlessness of shaving cream on his cheeks reminded him of her existence.

Now on his deck Stan waved his tongs at the bird that kept returning to the grill area despite the smoke rising from the sausages. "*Voertsek*," he said, Afrikaans for *Git!* He was glad of the diversion, because he was trying to think of something to talk about to his sons. "Look at this crazy bird, boys," he said, swatting at the blur that whizzed past his face. Kenneth, four, and Albert, six, were at the table playing a vicious card game, grabbing and slapping.

After only a few weekends Stan was starting to await his boys' visits with the same mixture of anticipation and dread he imagined a Japanese mother might feel on feast days as she prepared to dress her child's grave effigy in a new outfit the same size the child would have worn if it had still been alive. So lost was Stan in this last morbid thought that he did not consider the consequences when Albert said, "I can't see any bird, Dad—the sun is in my eyes." Stan let down the bamboo shade, only noticing the nest in its rolled recesses at the moment when the unfolding fabric no longer supported the untidy cluster of twigs and down. Three blind and naked hatchlings were ejected onto the heated wire grid where they writhed squeakily next to the sausages. The nest, too, bounced onto the grill and caught fire. Stan lobbed the burning knot of sticks and feathers onto the deck. The boys jumped up and gleefully stomped out the flames, giving Stan the chance to pick the twitching birds off the hot metal bars and toss them into the neighbor's yard before the boys could notice.

To Stan the dry, epidermal smell of flesh on hot metal seemed urgently and definingly African.

Later the same afternoon Stan and his boys were in the front row of Barnum and Bailey's Three Ring Circus. Stan's research assistant, Wendy, had surprised Stan with three tickets. Just over a month earlier Cecilia had been witness to Stan and Wendy's athletic performance on a quilt spread on Stan's office floor. Wendy, who was trying to atone for her role in the resulting unhappiness, had seen on TV that a Zulu dance troupe was touring with the circus, and had made reservations before the commercial was even over. "For father and sons," she had said in her quaint English, for she too was an immigrant.

Now they were in the Salt Palace arena, in the front row, dressed in identical T-shirts which displayed Mandela's portrait

and the inscription *Africa: my roots, my soul.* Stan put an arm about
each of his boys, and provided a commentary on the extravaganza
of Zulu warriors in leopard skin aprons high-kicking in the center
ring. "They're called *impis*," he told Albert. "It's a Zulu word for
soldier." The hypnotic beat of the drums, he elaborated, was
exactly as Stan had heard it from the servants' quarters on Saturday nights while he was growing up on his family's farm in the
Transvaal. He recognized snatches of a tune woven into the song,
and hummed along in Kenneth's ear: *We are marching to Pretoria,
Pretoria, Pretoria.*

For Stan the moment was whole. He gave the boys' shoulders a simultaneous squeeze, then leaned back in his seat relaxed.
In the ring before him the dancers responded to a slowing of the
drumbeat. They broke into a two-pronged formation, then
formed lines that snaked in and out of each other. Darkly glinting bodies intermingled as interchangeably as those that had
populated Stan's childhood.

Like many South African farm children, Stan had had black
friends. Stan now thought calling them friends was an overstate-
ment. For doesn't friendship imply mutuality?, and wasn't Stan in
his childhood games always the one who got to pull the trigger
and the black playmate of the day always the one to vie with the
dogs in mud or thorns for the honor of retrieving the wounded
bird?

In the middle ring the snake dance had come to an end. So
had the boys' patience. Albert wanted the clowns to be on again
and Kenneth was waiting for the Alligator Man, and between

them they had spilled a sack of popcorn and an orange drink. Stan's gaze was fixed momentarily between and around his shoes, where puffy popcorn clouds appeared to float over a sunset ocean. He did not see the dancers break formation and scatter from the hub of the stage as if along the spokes of a wheel, one of which intersected the rim at the point where Stan was sitting with his boys. When Stan again looked up his eyes were level with the bloodshot eyes of a large Zulu who, as Stan saw with his peripheral vision, was poised with his spear held overhead, ready to strike.

"Get down," Stan shouted to his boys. Albert clamped his arms around Stan's neck, and Kenneth raised his Dumbo flashlight overhead in an imitation of the Zulu's pose.

The impi raised himself to full height. He towered over Stan and the boys. The smell of sweat and marijuana hung in the space around his body. His face broke into a smile, baring an uneven set of teeth. He laughed—raucous guffaws, punctuated by bouts of hissing—and Stan was sprinkled with droplets of spit. At last the man pulled himself together. With a yip and a whistle he juggled his spear from one hand to the other, then held it behind his back. "You wear Mandela on your shirt," the man said. "You are girded with the armor of peace."

The man pulled away. He jogged to the exit with the rest of his troupe, shaking his head, apparently in wonder. Stan, shaking too, but over his whole body and involuntarily, could not even begin to assign emotional causes to his tremor.

Stan decided not to stay for the Alligator Man. He gathered his boys to go home. As he sat revving his car in the Salt Palace parking lot, "home" seemed as ambiguous to him as it used to be when, as a teenager, he vacillated between boarding school and the farm. At school his heart resided in the shape of Henrietta or her later avatars. At the farm a certain house maid was in a much more carnal fashion associated with the circulation of his blood.

It was during the winter vacation of his Matric year that Stan came home from boarding school to find two Marias working in the house, one in charge of the cleaning and the other in charge of the laundry. On Stan's Highveld farm the blacks did not have last names. First names were flexible too. So, after several days of confusion, Stan's mother changed the laundry-Maria's name to Hettie. An unfortunate coincidence: Hettie is short for Henrietta. Stan was then newly infatuated with Henrietta, and on his return to the hostel after the winter vacation, he would again exchange light signals with her (but not much more). In the case of the laundry-Hettie, Stan's exchanges were more substantial, if substantial is taken in the sense of physical materiality, as in body fluids, rather than in the sense of nonillusionistically, as in the keeping of promises.

In the afternoons when Stan's mother taught sewing at the black school and his father inspected the borehole pumps, Stan studied for his upcoming Mock Matric. He studied, that is, until the smell of hot metal on cotton made him check on Hettie's thoroughness. For if she missed even one spot on a towel or a pair of underpants, moth larvae could survive, could burrow under the epidermis and erupt after gorging on human flesh. While instructing Hettie about these hazards, Stan induced her to participate in a series of sex acts whose danger was ever after evoked for him by the hiss of a licked finger touched to a hot iron.

It struck Stan, as he spiraled down the off-ramp to Wendy's place, that participation might be too strong a word for Hettie's role in their activities. (But remember: those were the days before we had been acculturated to believe when a girl says "No" she means no. Not that Stan subscribed to the idea that *yes* or *no* was a foolproof indicator of acquiescence or refusal. Women rarely said no to him—and here I admit my share, but I was younger then. Wendy, again, was a different case: she apparently never said "No" to anybody. As Stan cannot refrain from mentioning, Wendy is not the type he usually falls for. His lack of elaboration hints that she is unremarkable; I infer she might even be downright unattractive. In fact, if he had not heard from Lueder and others about her talents in areas where looks do not matter, he would probably never have thought to associate with her other than professionally.)

Wendy was sitting on her living room floor amid sections of the paper. She pressed her empty coffee mug against her cheek, savoring its heat or its texture. Her gesture emphasized the broadness of her nose. Wendy's name was not really Wendy, but Nguyen Thi Kim Than. By the time, however, when Wendy knew enough English to explain that Nguyen Thi was in fact her family name, everyone, including Stan, was used to calling her Wendy.

"Boys," Stan now said, "this is Wendy. Say thank you for the circus tickets."

"A black man at the circus wanted to kill us," Albert said.

Wendy looked gravely from Stan to his boys. "When I was a little girl," she said, "I went with my father one year to the dead grass burning event."

"A nest caught on fire at my dad's house," Kenneth said.

Ignoring the interruption, Wendy continued. "It was a perfect evening for it. The sun was just setting, and a mist was moving over the venerable peak of Fan Si Pan. A flock of cranes flew by in a V-shaped formation. 'Look Father,' I said. My father looked. In an instant he grabbed me and rolled with me into the long grass and covered my body with his."

"He is ugly," Albert said. "He stinks." His speech was indistinct, because, fingers in his mouth, he was pulling his lips toward his nose in an ugly face.

"My father grew up in the war," Wendy said.

"Randy has a gun," said Kenneth. He shined his Dumbo flashlight on Wendy while imitating a strafing sound. Then he turned his flashlight onto his brother. Albert pulled his eyes into slits, lifting their outer corners upward. "Now you look like Wendy," Kenneth said.

Stan, still trying to clarify what had happened to him at the circus, said, "It wasn't just the boys. I was terrified too. I don't understand where the boys—they shouldn't be scared of blacks. Albert was just a baby when we left."

Albert stuck out a limp and drooling tongue. "Now I'm a retard."

"Clap," Wendy said. She meant crap. From the way she mixed up her l's and r's Stan knew something must have upset her.

"Clap," she said again. "Your boys will be scared of Mickey

Mouse unress you teach them not to be scared." She hit Stan harder than playfully in the chest. That instant, as he stared watery-eyed at the upside-down T-shirt image of Mandela, it came to Stan what a despicable human being he was, and how suitable was the epithet Cecilia had spat at him when she had discovered him with Wendy on his office floor. She had not said, "How dare you on my grandmother's quilt that she made out of blanket scraps from the Boer War concentration camp" (although she could have, because that was the quilt); instead she called him a *meidenaaier,* a noun so terrible that even P. W. Botha, the South African president who repealed the Immorality Act— thereby decriminalizing sexual intercourse across color lines— forced the Rapport Prize committee to take back the ten thousand rand they had already awarded Koos Prinsloo for his short story collection *Die Hemel Help Ons (Heaven Help Us)* when he, Botha, discovered the word had been used in one of those stories to describe the South African president himself.

"I need to use the VCR," Stan said to Cecilia when he took his boys home. This time "home" was the house he used to share with his soon-to-be ex-wife. The boys had run on ahead, while Stan had sat in the car, apostrophizing the TV antenna on Cecilia's roof for reasons to follow them. The VCR had been an inspiration. He had discovered a videotape in the glove compartment. The tape must have been there ever since he'd bought the car from Lueder. Cecilia looked suspicious. She also looked fresh out of the shower. Her hair made wet splotches on her T-shirt. She smelled of a vanilla wafer dipped into warm milk.

"As you know," Stan said, hoping he sounded inconvenienced, "I don't have a VCR." When he left, Cecilia had let him take only a sleeping bag. (He had not pressed the issue; he was then incapable of imagining the extent to which Cecilia would harden her heart.) "I have to do my research for that convention next week."

"The one in Las Vegas?" Cecilia asked. Scorn tightened her lips so they looked as if they needed to be softened by a kiss.

Kenneth appeared in the doorway. He held up a plastic shield. Albert was behind him. "Tell him that's just plastic, Dad," he said. "He's such a dork—he thinks a spear won't go through it."

"What have you done to the boys?" Cecilia said. "Kenneth was wailing about someone wanting to kill him."

"It was a coincidence."

"Daddy," Kenneth wailed. He clung to Stan's legs. "I want you to get a gun. Randy has a gun."

Stan picked him up. He drummed his knuckles on the shield. "Strong plastic. Who is Randy?"

He did not have to wait for Kenneth's answer to figure it out: a flush spread from Cecilia's cheeks to her neck. She turned her back on him and walked out. Stan tried to follow, but he was slowed down by Kenneth, who clung to his hair, and Albert, who had latched himself to his leg. He heard a door slam, the door to the bedroom he once shared with Cecilia, now closed against him. He was sure it stood open when the Randy guy with the gun was around.

The boys were crying. Stan picked Albert up too, carried the boys to the living room, and dropped them onto the couch. He slid the tape into the VCR. Carl Sagan flickered onto the screen. To the strains of the Pachelbel canon, Sagan exalted the cosmos. The music evoked in Stan a nostalgia so deep it seemed to reach back to the forsaken beginnings of the universe now being replayed on the screen. "Ridiculous," Stan thought, "Cecilia is a pacifist."

He sat down in a chair, comforting and known, and gathered his boys into his lap. In South Africa, when he was growing up, mothers were the ones who held boys on their laps. Back then science had incontrovertibly proven that fathers who were physical made their sons homosexuals, and a homosexual was the one thing worse than a *meidenaaier*, a fucker of black servant women. This latter was the epithet that had caused Stan's father, after he had been arrested under the Immorality Act and escaped, to jump to his death from the steeple of the Dutch Reformed Church near Stan's school, at that time the tallest structure with roof access in Pretoria. Stan received the news during Mock Matric, while he was writing his Biology exam.

The boys stopped crying. Stan wrestled them to the floor in an indulgence of roughhousing that would leave no doubt in their minds as to the kinds of interactions appropriate among men. Sometimes Stan worried about Albert: he was so highstrung; he was scared of everything. Someone might just seduce him with a gun. Dammit, Stan thought, I'll buy my own gun—I'll buy the boy a gun—I'll buy the boy a dog. He nuzzled up to Albert and growled. In the background Carl Sagan's voice rose over a crescendo of rousing music.

"Look boys," Stan said. The three of them lay panting on the carpet. "Voyagers I and II. They blasted off before either of you were born, and they're still going. Isn't that something?"

"It's dark out there," Albert said.

"The stars make light for them," Stan said. "See how they light up when they go by a star."

"Tonight I'm going to sleep with my flashlight on," said Kenneth.

On the TV humpback whales lamented. Carl Sagan commented in a voice-over: "Affixed to each of the Voyagers is a gold-plated disc bearing greetings from the planet Earth. Sixty human languages are represented, as well as the love songs of the humpback whales." The sound of the whales' songs caused Stan the same physical discomfort as the sound he managed to coax from a wineglass when he rubbed the rim until it wailed—an activity he was unable to resist no matter how repugnant he found its outcome.

The tape played on, the boys fell asleep. Cecilia spoke from the hallway end of the room. "Research for a presentation?" she asked.

"You let some cowboy be around my boys with a gun."

Again Cecilia turned away from Stan. A shudder of disdain traveled from her shoulders to her butt. As good a place as any, Stan thought, from which to start fucking her back to her senses.

When Stan carried his boys to their bedroom, he took heart from the fact that Cecilia was waiting there, pulling away the covers. She could watch him being a good father. He kissed Kenneth, who opened his eyes and said, "Dumbo is a retard."

Stan attempted to catch Cecilia's eye, but she looked

resolutely at the wallpaper. Kenneth had inherited Cecilia's ability to drop instantly into a deep sleep. And, like Cecilia, he spoke his dreams aloud when he was disturbed. On the first night of Cecilia and Stan's honeymoon, Stan had gone out onto the balcony to smoke a cigarette in order to allow Cecilia time to prepare herself for their physical union. He felt it necessary to be that considerate since he assumed she was a virgin. He would have to wait till the next morning to find out if his assumption had been correct, because when he returned Cecilia had fallen into what he later learned to recognize as one of those sleeps from which it was impossible to rouse her. For one moment that night Stan thought Cecilia was responding. She had opened her eyes and said, "Rawalpindi to Chittagong," an expression so brimful with exotic promise that it took all of Stan's willpower not to give in to his enflamed desire without her waking participation.

At Kenneth's bedside more than a decade after his honeymoon, Stan was subject to a similar desire. But as we live and learn, he had no expectation of having it fulfilled as rapidly as before. Everything is relative, Stan thought, since he never in his hot-blooded days imagined "rapidly" would be a suitable adverb to use in connection with his wedding night. Such were his thoughts when Cecilia moved toward him.

"Randy isn't a cowboy," she said. "He's a geologist. He's teaching them gun safety. At least he's teaching them *something*."

BILLY MXENGE

After making inquiries at the circus trucks parked outside the Salt Palace, Stan had found the motel where the Zulu dancers were staying. On the second-storey deck overlooking the parking lot, a bunch of blacks had gathered. Stan thought they had to be Zulus, but couldn't tell because they were wearing jeans and T-shirts or sports jackets. When he got out of his car, one of them hailed him by yelling, "Mandela's friend is my friend." It was the man who had singled Stan out of the crowd at the circus. He had been leaning against the deck railing at some distance from the others. He had tossed down a beer, which Stan had managed to catch in a rugby dive that earned him the applause of the onlookers.

Now Stan was sitting next to his new acquaintance, who had introduced himself as Billy. Billy had his feet on the railing, and was comparing the pink sunset over the Great Salt Lake with the spectacle at Lake Kariba where six million flamingoes gathered every year to mate. Billy had witnessed this phenomenon during his exile from South Africa, a period in which he had also received training as a revolutionary soldier.

"How come they threw you out of the country?" Stan asked. He was using a tightly rolled dollar note to work the condensation on his beer bottle into coherent rivulets.

Billy downed the remainder of his beer and settled back expansively. After a thought-gathering silence, he started to tell the story of his childhood. Like Stan, he grew up on a South African farm. Together they reminisced about barefoot sorties along mud-bogged footpaths to plunder weaverbirds' nests; revisited the throat-smarting sourness of the wild marula fruit; and traded anecdotes about the dangerous pleasure of smoking out bees with a dung-fueled torch. As soon as Billy's tale touched on his social exploits, however, Stan started to understand that their childhood experiences had, in fact, been worlds apart. While Stan boarded the elementary school bus with the other white children each day to learn about the Nile Delta or the Eiffel Tower, Billy (whose parents could not afford the black school's fees) and some similarly impoverished friends busied themselves around the farms where their parents worked with various acts of sabotage. This experience came in handy, Billy said, when, as an adolescent, he became a revolutionary. As he cited examples of his skills, Stan started to think in a new light of the many inexplicable failures that used to plague the equipment on his own father's farm.

Unaware of the suspicion he had cast on Stan's playmates, Billy continued. So closely did his transgressive acts border on accident, he explained, that it was not until he was a man—which in Billy's tribe comes with proof of one's first ejaculation—that a series of these unfortunate incidents "broke the proverbial camel's back." That's how Billy said it. Stan was surprised. He complimented Billy on his idiomatic English usage, and Billy told him it was in his years of exile that he had learned to read and write English as well as his mother tongue, Xhosa. He was actually a Xhosa, he reiterated, winking to suggest his tribal origin had something to do with the distance he was keeping from the other dancers, who, he explained, were actually Zulus. Pointing to Stan's shirt, he added proudly that he was related to Nelson Mandela. As to what he was doing with a Zulu dance troupe, Billy answered with a shrug of the shoulders: "Let's say I had to leave the country in a hurry."

The truth was, Billy had a long history of suddenly having to leave the country in a hurry. It appeared that he owed even his present name to his extensive stay in foreign parts. Billy, Billy explained, was a literary allusion: it was the name given his cock by the same lover who'd introduced him to a children's classic, "Three Billy Goats Gruff." It was this lover, Billy said, who had set fire to the only car he'd ever owned, a white Mercedes he'd bought from some Jew who had to leave Zambia in a hurry.

"Cash," Billy said. "Damn, that was a nice car." He sighed.

"Who has a nice car?" A woman two doors down tossed her cigarette onto the deck and stepped on it with the toe of her sandal.

"Him," Stan and Billy said at the same time, each pointing at the other.

The woman laughed. Her voice seemed too deep-toned for her slight body. She walked over, introduced herself, and sat down on the bench between them. Her name was Myra. She was in town for a conference. Her blond hair was pulled into a ponytail so tight her scalp shone through pink above her ear. When, elbows on knees, she leaned forward to study the view, the vee of her dress buckled at the neck, revealing a turquoise strap that cut into her shoulder under an alarming weight of breast. She motioned toward the fire escape where a number of dancers were sitting with their beers. "You from some sports team?" she asked.

"Yes," Billy said. He reached past Myra to point at Mandela's picture on Stan's chest. He winked. "We're on Winnie's football team."

Stan handed Myra a beer. Someone on the fire escape intoned an a capella song, and some of the other dancers picked up the tune. It was the same sound that used to drift, when Stan was a child, from the workers' shacks into the farmhouse, and it was now—thanks to Paul Simon's *Graceland*—a sound with geographical specificity to many Americans. Myra looked from Stan's shirt to the singers, put two and two together, and said, "You're from South Africa."

"He is," Billy and Stan said at the same time, pointing once again. They lifted their beers and clinked them over Myra's head. "A good place to be from, I hear," Myra said. She emphasized the *from*.

Stan had modeled his adult years on the assumption that what Myra had just said was true. Lately, though, he had become aware that for him there would always be a *here* and a *there*, and that his heart was *there* as often as it was *here*. Emigration had not succeeded in ridding him of some peculiarly African ghosts. They seemed to have emigrated with him. And, right then, their insubstantial shapes were inspissated by the scent of this woman and the melancholy tones of that Zulu song. *To the banks of the Magalakwini the bushbuck come at dawn and dusk to feed on the nourishing roots of the waterlilies.*

"Things are changing," Billy said. "Soon it will be our turn."

"I hear they're letting Mandela out," Myra said. "Imagine: a face no one has seen for as long as I've lived."

"Isn't that something," Stan said. "His wife waited for him twenty-seven years."

"My husband didn't even wait twenty-seven months."

"I can relate to that."

"You two been to jail?" Billy asked.

"Only in a manner of speaking," Myra said. "I'm in medical school. My husband bailed after my first year. He got too lonely. On the nights when I did make it home, he didn't want me to come near him. He couldn't stand the smell of embalming fluid."

Billy lifted Myra's hand to his face and inhaled. "Medical school," he said. "Hey Stan, Myra is a doctor. You got a pain, she'll fix it."

"Not a doctor yet," Myra said, and pulled her hand from Billy's.

"I was almost a doctor once," Stan said. "When I was a student I was a medic at the mines. I still remember this from the *Miner's Companion:* 'If you suffer a penetrating wound of the joint with fluid and blood escaping, report to the nearest European.'"

Billy laughed. "Sounds like the *Lover's Companion* to me," he said. He eyed Myra's body, lingering at the point where her thighs exited her tight skirt. "See, in South Africa you would be able to doctor blacks already."

Myra tugged loose a thread from her hem. Stan took his pocketknife, pulled out the blade, leaned over, and took the thread from her fingers. As he nicked it off, he thought, The everlastingness of embalming fluid. "Did you know the Egyptians used to preserve dead babies in honey?"

"Honey instead of formaldehyde—that could have saved my marriage."

"In my experience," Billy said, "it's over when it's over. Take Nelson and Winnie for example. I have it from reliable sources that she has something going on the side."

"Why wait twenty-seven years and fuck it up now?" Stan asked. He stood up and leaned against the railing.

"You have to see it from her point of view. A young woman with needs." Billy took Myra's hand once more, and placed it on his chest in the position Americans use to pledge allegiance to their flag. He held it there, cupping Myra's elbow in his hand. He bent over to set down his beer bottle, and as he came to an upright position, he trailed the fingers of his other hand across her leg. "Hmmm," he said. His evaluative hum changed into a throaty rumble, which he wove into the chorus of voices from the fire escape.

Myra hummed along like someone who was trying hard to remember the words. She looked at the singers. Next she looked toward Stan. Then she pulled away her arm. Or tried to. But since Billy held it at the elbow, she was able to execute only the first half of a beckoning wave.

Stan clenched his hands around the railing. In the last light of dusk he saw Billy take hold of Myra's head, bring her face up to his, and kiss her slowly on the lips. As he kissed Myra, Billy stared directly into Stan's eyes. That instant it was as if Stan saw the contact print of a negative he had carried about with him for years but had never once held up to the light. Billy, Stan thought, has seen into the darkness of my heart.

Myra freed her hand, pulled her face away, and whimpered.

She got to her feet, grabbed her beer bottle with both hands like a club, and swung it back for maximum momentum. Stan had come forward to do something—to punch Billy's fat lips, maybe—so it was his shoulder and his temple that deflected the bottle from its arced path. A meteorite of pain illuminated the space behind Stan's eyelids. When the magnesium brightness faded, the first thing Stan saw was Billy's expression of wide-eyed fear. Stan had the momentary satisfaction of thinking his approach had caused it, but the focus of Billy's gaze made him think again. He turned around, and faced, for the second time that day, a Zulu brandishing a traditional weapon: this man, though, was armed with a broken bottle. "Billy," the man said, "you giving us Zulus a bad name again." Behind him, backed up to the fire escape, a throng of men blocked the way out.

Stan put his hand in his pocket to feel for his car keys. The Zulu interpreted his move as a signal to act. He swung. Now it was Billy who intercepted the blow. Like a gymnast going for the crossbar, Billy leaped. Both he and his assailant went down to the sound of grinding glass. Once down, Billy rolled to the edge of the balcony and squeezed under the railing. He dropped from sight.

After Myra had screamed, "Catch him, catch him"; after Stan had run down the stairs to the parking lot; after bottles had rained down around him and Billy; after Billy had shouted, "Hey you Zulus, Mandela is going to be your king," and, "I spit on the face of King Goodwill Zweletini's number one wife," and, "I spit on the face of King Goodwill Zweletini's number two wife"; and after both men had reached Stan's car, and after Stan had pulled away with engine roaring and tires screeching, Billy leaned back in his seat. His laugh was a resonant boom that filled the car like a stereo. When he could speak again, Billy said, "Wathinta abafasi, wathimta imbokotho uzakufa."

"What does it mean?" Stan asked. "My only Xhosa is from the *Miner's Companion*."

Billy, systematically searching the pockets of his sports coat, answered, "If you strike a woman, you have struck a rock, and you will die."

"This woman," Stan said, "the one who burned your car— what did you do to her?"

"Before or after?" Billy was absorbed in rolling a joint which he then lit and drew from before passing it to Stan.

Stan sucked the sweet smoke and allowed his imagination to supply the particulars of who did what to whom, a task he performed tolerably well, since he had his own memories of a decisive moment when putting out a fire was no longer an option:

On the night after his father's funeral, Stan had gone home to his family's farm. He was the man of the house now. The district sergeant had had the foresight to warn him that some of the neighboring farmers might be inclined to demonstrate that the kind of thing his father died of would not be tolerated in their area. The sergeant did not think it would come to anything more than a few bricks on the roof. Or maybe one or two rocks through the windows. This was why Stan was awake, clutching his father's .22 when a rap came at his bedroom window soon after midnight.

As it turned out, the police sergeant's fear of white vengeance may have been only a voicing of his own dark fantasies: Stan had his hands full with the results of vengeance from the other end of the color spectrum. No white face appeared in the window rectangle: a black one did. In his sleep-deprived state, though, the differentiation by color struck Stan as somehow absurd, since Maria/Hettie was curiously drained of color when she mouthed, "Baas, please help me!" before dropping out of sight.

It was Hettie's brothers who had subjected her to a vaginal equivalent of washing a child's mouth out with soap. Substituting battery acid, they had applied their prophylactic when she confessed to being pregnant—either by the big boss or the little boss, she could not say which. Their ad hoc abortifacient was still present in sufficient quantity between Hettie's legs to erode a hole in the sleeve of Stan's pajama shirt when he picked Hettie up from among the cannas.

In the hours that followed, Stan offered whatever he could find on the pantry shelves to alleviate Hettie's pain, the expression of which was fortunately circumscribed by frequent bouts of fainting. Near morning, when she came to consciousness with an unguarded scream, the noise brought Stan's mother to the scene with paraffin lantern held high like some Florence Nightingale on-the-veld. She started to anoint him and Hettie with an aromatic liquid shaken from a bottle. Only when his mother broke the lantern glass was Stan thoroughly awakened. He then recognized the liquid as the highly flammable one used for dry cleaning. At the moment of his illumination, Stan was able to tear off his doused pajama shirt and toss it back toward his mother. She was, just then, applying the exposed flame of the lamp to Hettie, who had sunk into another faint. The shirt covered both women like a shared prayer shawl. A mandorla of flames leaped around their heads. Stan's mother was shouting something. But it wasn't a prayer. She was repeating the epithet *meidenaaier.*

This was the word that drove Stan away, so that he was outside the house by the time the flames reached the propane tank that once fueled Hettie's iron.

WHERE I COME IN

Stan and Billy had stopped for a drink or two, and were now on their way to borrow a sleeping bag from Wendy. At Wendy's apartment the parking spot Stan had come to think of as his was occupied. He parked his car behind the usurper, and revved the engine desultorily.

"The man who is fucking with your woman?"

"No," Stan said. "This isn't my woman's—my wife's place." He got out and walked around the offending vehicle. It was Lueder's car. "It's the other woman who lives here."

"Is he fucking with your other woman also?"

Stan did not reply. He reached past Billy to the glove compartment. "Do you know who Carl Sagan is?"

"Is he also fucking with your other woman?"

"He's a scientist. He did this thing on TV about the universe—where it all comes from and where it's going."

"No TV in Mbokolo," Billy said. "So where does it come from and where is it going?"

"He doesn't really say," Stan said. "Nobody really knows. He's just giving his best guess."

"If the man doesn't have the answers, why doesn't he shut the fuck up?" Billy said.

"Good point." Stan brandished the videotape in front of Billy's face. "Come," he said. "I'm going to give this tape back to the man it belongs to." He stuck his finger through the two inches of exposed tape and pulled.

But for the first time since he'd known her, Wendy said "No." No she wouldn't fetch Lueder so they could stuff the tape up his ass; no she wouldn't lend them a sleeping bag. In the face of such rejection, all Stan could think of was to plug the exhaust of Lueder's car with tape and pieces of the box. When there was some tape left over, Billy had the idea of wadding it into the other orifices under the hood. Once done, Stan admitted he had a problem with America. "It's too goddamn civilized," he said.

Billy empathized. "It's not the same," he said. "That bang when it gets to the fuel tank."

"No," said Stan. "It's not the same. How many wives does King Goodwill have now, anyway?"

"He was up to five last I heard," Billy said. "I'm not going to like it much living here."

"You're going to live here?" Stan asked.

"Of course," Billy said. "You think those Zulus are ever going to take me back? They going to kill me."

Stan returned to the car to think about this. So did Billy. They sat in silence like old friends, or people married a long time. And there I will leave them for the time being, each to ponder in his own way questions that may or may not have answers. For despite Stan's and Billy's separate skepticisms, the asking of questions is an important activity in itself. After all, didn't Carl Sagan quote John Wheeler, physicist, who said the deepest lesson of quantum mechanics may be that reality is defined by the questions we put to it?

This is my story: I was seventeen, white, an Afrikaner of a philosophical bent, who liked to read Ayn Rand and Thomas Mann. I knew Descartes' three arguments for the existence of God and could point out the logical fallacies in each of them. I was able to read in four languages, including Latin, and one day, when I was studying in the library my all girls' school shared with our brother school across the road, a Matric boy with the face of the Hermes of Andros came up to me and said, "You look like someone who'd know what *Scribit ad narrandum, non ad probandum* means." And I did, and I told him. He thanked me, walked away, and did not speak another word to me until ten years later when we met under very different circumstances. Thus I knew the world, both ancient and modern, though mostly from books.

Within hours of leaving that milieu for the first time—I was seventeen, on my way to America as an exchange student—I found myself in an airplane stranded on the single runway of the Nouakchott International Airport, a stone's throw away from the city of Nouakchott, capital of the Islamic Republic of Mauritania. I and the rest of the planeload of people were awaiting the arrival of an engine part being flown from the legendary city of

Timbouctoo, a thousand miles away in neighboring Mali. It was hot. The South African passengers were all whites—South African blacks did not travel in those days. Holders of South African passports were not allowed to get off the plane. In the seat next to me sat an exchange student we'd picked up in Nigeria. His name was Lawrence Ouma, and he'd been in and out of the plane, chatting to the guard at the open door. He returned from time to time with glasses of sweet tea. He handed these around as a sign of goodwill and solidarity. In between these sallies he balanced a chess board between our seats and we played. He was a slow thinker, so I had time to study his head and his naked torso. He had taken his shirt off because of the heat. I was able to conclude he could have been the model for Antico's bronze and gold statue of Meleager—hero of Aetolia—except for its hair of gold; for Lawrence was a shiny black, from the top of his molded Afro to the pinch of his belly button, a black with the patina of wood often handled, like the black knight trembling between my fingers.

Remember: I was seventeen, and never been kissed.

I excused myself and went to the toilet. I wanted to wash my hands and my arm where his had touched it. But the plane had run out of water and the toilet had begun to stink. So instead I squeezed my pimples until my face assumed a shameful permanent blush. I stuck a patch of licked toilet paper on a bleeding spot on my forehead. When I decided to return, two boys from my brother school waited for me at the door. They blocked the way back to my seat. "We play chess too," they said. They pushed me into the galley and drew the curtain. Reaching under my shirt and under my bra, they each grabbed hold of a breast. "We want some of what's so cheap you're giving it to that kaffir," the freckled one said. I struggled to get away, but I did not scream, because I knew I deserved it. A few seconds later the turbaned guard pushed aside the curtain with the barrel of his gun and motioned for us to get back to our seats. I followed the boys down the aisle. But when I got to the plane's open door, I ran toward the rectangle of sky hanging over the airport building. I tripped down the stairs into a strange light. A crescent moon was stenciled on the gable of the terminal building. It was shortly after noon, June 7, 1973. Although I did not know it when I stumbled onto the tarmac, I was about to witness the longest total solar eclipse in recorded history.

I blundered into a run, tripping over my shadow as it skimmed across the potholes of a deserted road. The road led away from the airport, away from the gloomy cluster of buildings that was the city of Nouakchott. When it became obvious I wasn't being followed, I slowed to a brisk walk and sucked moisture from my cheeks to swallow away the sting in my throat. Drawn by the sound of drums, I left the road. I clambered up a sandy incline, using tussocks of grass as hand- and footholds. When I reached the top, there was a beach before me, a pewter ocean stretching behind it. Seminaked figures were beating with brooms on the hulls of upturned boats. I steadied myself against the trunk of a tree. Its shade on my skin was an eerie purple. So was my own shadow against the sand. I looked up. There were no clouds. In the sun's place was a crescent no larger than the arc of Islam's moon.

I knew what it was. I had read the astronomy magazine our school subscribed to from England. At first, as the light around me dimmed to the intensity of bright moonlight, I tried to remember terms and definitions: umbra and penumbra, the length of the saros, Bailey's beads. But when a black hole took the place of the sun, I watched with an awe disconnected from words. Venus emerged on the horizon. The cry of a muezzin sounded.

This I forgot to tell: I'm very religious. A strange thing to leave out, you may think. But no. Do you mention, when you tell people about yourself, that you breathe? I was religious then too, but with a self-punishing piety that led me to despise Martin Luther, to whose principles the Dutch Reformed Church I grew up in adhered, for having abolished the practice of self-flagellation. My religious convictions now? We'll get to now later.

I ran down the incline, pulling off my shirt as I went. Bra and skirt and panties followed, dropped on the beach as I ran. At water's edge I sat down and took off my shoes. I flung myself down in the shallow surf, so that the breaking waves foamed around my breasts. Other figures joined me in the breakers. A woman squatted by me. She scooped up water in her hands and poured it over me. I felt the brush of her breasts against my back. She intoned a song, and the others picked up the melody. Their high voices reverberated in my skull. An abrupt sunrise erased the morning star. In the distance a cock crowed.

I lived a lifetime during that eclipse. I found out later totality had lasted five minutes and thirty-two seconds, but at the time duration had no meaning for me. Many things have happened between then and now; none of them, though, has obliterated the impact on my mind of a world dissolved into monochromatic sterility at midday, a world etched with doom. After a long, long time, daylight restored a blue-green shimmer to the ocean, bringing with it—hope. Although I was only seventeen, this was my Damascus moment. The soil on which I knelt was African. And that is why, unlike Stan—whom I love like a brother—I will never leave this continent.

Stan, on the other hand, subscribes to the idea of new beginnings. He feels he should be able to put the past behind him, find a way to unlink the series of regrettable events that make up his life. In fact, Stan prefers not to think of the events of his life as a series, since (as he points out whenever our talk drifts into philosophy) the mere temporal succession of events or the spatial proximity of objects does not imply a causal connection. This is where I differ from Stan: I have to believe there is an order beyond reason. I have to believe there is a Power in whose hands the most tangled webs unsnarl themselves like the silken fringe of a tallith. I have to believe this, as I have to believe Stan's story will have a happy ending. Because, if reconciliation is not possible between Stan and Cecilia, how will it be possible between the millions and millions of wrongdoers and wronged in this country?

To return to Stan: after the strange meeting between him and Billy that day, he had the clear sensation of embarking on a new beginning. The fact that the side door of Cecilia's house happened to have been left unlocked that night, and that he and Billy managed to make their way inside without disturbing anyone—especially considering how drunk Billy was—bode well for a future that started fresh at that moment. He also thought it was an auspicious sign that when he took Billy to gaze with him upon his sleeping children Albert woke up and showed no fear. The boy reached for his baseball bat at the foot of his bed, and instead of using it to defend himself against Billy, he asked Billy to sign it. But the most propitious portent of the evening occurred when he helped Billy back past Cecilia's bedroom, helped him into the living room and onto the couch, pulled off his shoes, covered him with the concentration camp quilt, and Billy said, "Stan, you are my mother and my father arisen from the dead."

Stan returned to the bedroom and lay on the bed next to Cecilia. The springs creaked as he lowered himself. He felt that Cecilia acknowledged his presence when she lifted her head and said, "From eight to ten in the Kon-Tiki Lounge." Her head dropped back onto the pillow, and she turned on her side, with her back to him, pushing up a huge wave of blanket with her shoulder. *How profound the silence must be,* Stan thought, *in the everlasting night between the galaxies. How sweet to the beings of those distant worlds the glissandos of the humpback whales.*

And then he thrust out a leg and searched for her toes.

The Epistemology
of Romantic Despair

1. THAT SPACE

The reason it takes so long, Sylvie tells her mother, is that you have only one free choice. Once you pick the first object, everything that follows depends on it.

Meredith hears in Sylvie's statement the intimations of a great truth, but when she tries to grasp it, it uncoils like a serpent spitting out its tail. Deciding, for now, on the rapid edificatory power of wine, she crosses over to the refrigerator. For a moment she stands illuminated in the cold light streaming from its open door. The bottle of red she has been chilling a week and a day reminds her of a different failure, and besides it is only noon. So instead of the wine she takes out an egg and cracks it on the rim of the goblet. She gives the white to the cat, and shakes parsley and thyme into the yolk to make a potion for her face. Although it is a weekday and she is supposed to work, it feels like a holiday because her daughter Sylvie has stayed home from school. From her work corner in the dining room Meredith has been listening for Sylvie's pings and dongs instead of working. In the end she has given up and gone to the kitchen.

She now takes her egg mixture into her bedroom. After applying it, she lies on her bed awaiting the metamorphosis suggested by the elemental smell of sulphur in her nostrils: her head floats in earth, water, air, and fire. A sound comes from the other side of the house, like a hesitant voice, a clearing of the air. Note follows note in a rising sequence, a succession of compressions and rarefactions that carries energy into that space that goes on to the end of the world. But it is not Sylvie's voice Meredith hears; it is the pulses of sound, the throaty tones of objects being struck as Sylvie makes her soundscape.

2. SOFT ERROR

Meredith works for the nuclear power plant at the other end of town. She does her work on a terminal at home and only goes to the site once a week to confer with the project team. Even so, especially after what happened yesterday, Sylvie holds her personally responsible for the birth defects in Hiroshima, the dead sheep in Utah, and the decline of the honeybee in sub-Saharan Africa. Meredith feels like a delinquent migrant worker in McLuhan's global village.

She should have known: yesterday morning when she logged on and downloaded her data for the day, the printout resembled the transubstantiation of a devil's brain. Glossolalia in print: letters and words piled on and repeated in predictable but nevertheless incoherent ways. In a small way it had thrilled her. It had given her an excuse to phone Bill. Her colleague. The computer whiz. For him she has tracked down a Cape Town Shiraz in the local wine store and chilled it for eight days, because Bill, she believes, quizzed her with more than a wine connoisseur's interest when she mentioned liking her red wine refrigerated since that was how she had learned to drink it growing up in South Africa where there was no air-conditioning and summer indoor temperatures soared far above the comfort zone. After speculating about the effect of excessive heat on the malolactic fermentation process, Bill said he would like to try a cold South African red sometime. (So far she has not had the nerve to invite him.)

Bill? Has the computer been down?

Meredith.

There was nothing wrong with the system, he said. Must have been a *soft error.* "It's not like a burnt out circuit or a broken wire," he explained. "It's a different kind of malfunction. A tiny switch fails only once, like at the moment you are transmitting your data. Then it works again."

"So I don't have to come in? You don't have to fix it?"

"There's nothing to fix. It's just a quantum particle flying through one of the switches. God playing craps. One of those things that happen from time to time in the universe."

Meredith sat staring at her screen. *To hell with Einstein,* she thought. *God actually plays dice.* And just then God, that Crapulous Crapshooter, hit her with a throw that showed just how crappy/crabby He could be.

The doorbell rang. A black delivery truck with the logo *Sweet Revenge* was parked on the curb. The driver wore white vampire makeup and a black jogging suit. He held a cone of newspaper tied with a black ribbon out to Meredith. Something floriferous was visible at the top. Her first thought was that Sylvie was being asked for a dance. Dance-asking at her daughter's school was an elaborate affair. When Dave, who was now her boyfriend, asked her to the Halloween dance, he'd delivered a tombstone sculpted from cardboard at their door. *Rest in Peace*, it had said, *You Have Been Asked*. Inside was a plastic skeleton in pieces, which, when assembled, announced his name and phone number from top to bottom on either side down the ribs.

When Meredith folded back the paper from what the vampire had brought, she saw roses the hue of dried blood. In freshness they must have been the color of love, but now they were dead. Her hand slipped from the handle of the tightly sprung door, causing it to hit her hard against the funny bone. While waiting for the shards of pain to subside, she started wondering how dead roses might feature in an invitation. She read the card. *Roses are red / Some hearts are true. / I saw you with B—, / so: FUCK YOU.*

For an instant Meredith could only imagine that the sender was her soon-to-be ex-husband Ray. She experienced a brief exaltation, a high note of triumph that the impending finalization of her divorce, which had been proceeding in such a civilized manner, had at last gasp elicited a passionate gesture. Added to that was the delicious scenario that sprung instantly from the phrase, *I saw you with B—* In her mental image she saw it happening: Ray observing her and Bill in the power plant parking lot, their eyes (hers and Bill's) locked in an intimate glance. Never mind that it had never happened—the image satisfied her completely. But her momentary glee was erased when she saw that the card was addressed to Sylvie after all.

3. THE CHOKER

In glancing at this picture, you will probably at once see a young woman in three-quarter view, facing away to the left. On the other hand, you may be that one person in five who immediately sees an old hag facing to the left and forward: a hag whose mouth is made of the young woman's black choker. This picture has been constructed so that various of its details have a dual function. One may, upon contin-ued inspection of the ambiguous image, become adept at shifting from one way of organizing it to the other, but one can never organize it both ways at once. An important point is that unless we had told you that there was a second picture, you certainly would not have suspected it or looked for one.

She remembered that picture from her college psychology class.

Meredith/Sylvie.

Mother/daughter.

The one but not the other. She knew it was impossible to see everything at once. But Meredith is a mother, and it is her job to look for more than one story in every face she loves. So she stud-ied the florist's card some more. Although it was unsigned, it could be from no one other than Skeleton Dave, the boy with whom Sylvie had gone not only to the Halloween dance, but to Morp (which is Prom backwards, Meredith had learned), to the Christmas dance, and to Girl's Choice. She tried to imagine what could have elicited the macabre token of rejection she held in her hands. Twelve dead long-stemmed roses, a sincere intention to wound. It would have been excessive even for the ending of a marriage. And she had not even thought of Sylvie and Dave as having a *relationship*. They were having fun. They *went* together, they were *an item;* what used to be in Meredith's time *going steady, courting* in her mother's day. *Making love* when her grandmother was a girl. *A rose is a rose is a rose.*

Breaking up. They probably still call it breaking up. Sylvie had talked about this way of ending a relationship, when she was still mentioning things. "She sent him a mushroom, like, you know, the kind that smells like fish. 'You take up too mush room in my life.' Get it?" That had sounded funny in relation to a school friend of Sylvie: a name to Meredith, with no face attached. But this moldy-smelling caricature of a bouquet was for her daughter, her gentle-spirited Sylvie!

4. MUSICA MUNDANA

She decided to spirit away the flowers. Undo the act. As a matter of integrity she would later tell Sylvie about the delivery, but it would not be as bad as seeing. Or smelling. *The olfactory bulb is directly plugged into memory.* Meredith would turn back the wheel. Like a kind of smart angel in medieval cosmology, she would form "a Bridge betwene thinges Incorporeal and thinges naturall," would instantly transmute an ideal solution into the gross fabric of matter.

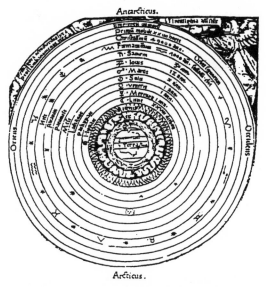

Musica mundana, the music of the universe. Illustration from Aristotle's *De caelo*, ed. Gedeon von Eck (Augsburg, 1519)

Thynges Mathematicall gyve Form to the base & grosse. All things which are, & have beyng, are found under a triple diversitie generall. For, either, they are demed Supernaturall, Naturall, or, of a third being: which, by a peculiar name also, are called Thynges Mathematicall. By Pythagoras his discoverie, beyng the Proportions of harmonie, Mathematicks is hable to signify the unchaungable and incorruptible tones of the Material universe. Earth, beyng base & grosse, soundeth the tone most base.

Earth, being base, needs math to translate its baseness into harmony. *Intelligentia assistes.* That's what she would be—that helpful creature between nature and God, in the upper right-hand corner of *Musica mundana*, music of the spheres. That's what Meredith would give: intelligent assistance. She is, she would say to those who would question her ontology, qualified: she has a Master's in Math.

She kept quiet for a while when Sylvie first came home. Sylvie was animated and announced she was making a soundscape out of *objets trouvé* for her *Proud to Be Me* self-esteem class. Before Meredith could stop her, she went outside to raid the outside garbage can for potentially melodic objects. Sylvie returned, not only bearing the crumbling material substance of the roses, but also a grudge of megascopic proportions.

You have no right to throw my stuff away.

I was thinking of your feelings.

You treat me like a child. You think I can't handle anything. Just because you cannot face the truth about your—

They smell rotten.

They're supposed *to.*

Then Sylvie blustered through the house banging closed all the doors between Meredith's work corner in the dining room and her bedroom. For the rest of the afternoon the only communication that passed between them was Sylvie's "I've GOT it" over the extension every time the phone rang. When the doorslamming in reverse order brought her once again into Meredith's presence, she stayed only long enough to say in a voice damped with crying, "I'm going with Kirstin." She ran outside and got into a car before Meredith could ask, "Who? When?"

When turned out to be very much later, when Meredith was already holding the phone in her hand to dial another round of

phone numbers she had found marked in Sylvie's school direc-
tory. She'd had to resort to that, because Sylvie was not with her
best friend Maren. Maren hadn't seen her. Meredith had gone
cold with fear when she'd heard that. The self-esteem assembly
had been the school's response to a suicide in Sylvie's grade. *Our
Counseling staff is not taking any chances,* the note had said. *These
things turn into epidemics.* In fact, by the time *when* came around,
Meredith was beside herself to the point of having decided to call
Sylvie's father.

Ray was not answering his phone. But close to midnight,
when Meredith was about to phone the police, he called from
Meredith's front door. "Everything's fine," he hollered. "Kooks
had a little accident." He led Sylvie in, fresh from the emergency
room. "Finger got caught in the door."

Sylvie was still not talking. Her finger splint pointed at her
mother in an accusatory way. "I'm dead," she said. And went to
her room.

Ray stood in the door.

"You could have called," Meredith said.

"Your phone was busy. Been talking to someone?"

She could see he was going to stay long enough to prove that
a year of separation had not blunted the skill with which he was
able to drill through her certainties and into the soft core of her
doubt. He, of course, had had a woman waiting in the wings
when they'd separated. In fact, even before there was talk of
divorce he had grown a wart on his ring finger *so that his wedding
band did not fit.* Meredith could read these signs like an augur.

"Bummer," he said, "about Maren."

She was forced to ask, to admit she did not know anything. He told—chosen parent that he was—what he had learned in the confidence-sharing milieu of the emergency room. Maren and Dead Roses Dave were now an item. Maren had comforted Dave during Sylvie's alleged straying to Brad.

Oh, B—, Meredith thought. With this association unleashed, her thoughts sped ahead. Bill had a son. She had once seen them, together, carrying a box through the parking lot. They'd laughed and talked. "You seem to have a good relationship," Meredith had remarked. "That's easy," Bill had said. "He lives with his mother."

It was Maren, Ray said, who had slammed the door on Sylvie's finger. It was no accident, he thought. "Do you think we should sue?"

His use of "we" collapsed Meredith's anger. Better, she said, that Sylvie not suspect someone would deliberately hurt her.

5. Broca's aphasia

Meredith hears a liquid sound when she wakes up from her nap. She remembers Sylvie did not go to school. Her finger ached, she'd said. Meredith remembers the egg yolk mask she'd applied. It has tightened around her nose and cheeks like a balloon pulled over her face. She slides her fingers over its plastic surface. When she crunches up her nose, the mask becomes rough with hairline fractures. She pulls it off in yellow shreds, then washes her face. Her skin feels smooth, rejuvenated. Smile becomes choker. Hag morphs to girl.

She goes to the kitchen. Sylvie is still working on her sound-scape. "Tea?" Meredith asks. Sylvie shakes her head no. Meredith makes herself a cup. She pulls out a chair at the table. There's no room to put down her tea, because Sylvie's junk is scattered unappetizingly across the whole surface. Meredith is careful not to appear inconvenienced, because she is relieved to see Sylvie take an interest in something.

She herself feels upbeat. *The healing cave of sleep.* She feels loquacious. "Quite a project you have going here."

Sylvie only has ears for the pings emitted by her lengths of pipe, her empty bottles, her soil-damped tins. The lines of concentration on Sylvie's face are too intense to be real, Meredith thinks. "I know some stuff about tuning," Meredith says.

Ting.

"The sound an object makes depends on how fast it vibrates."

Dong.

At times like this Sylvie reminds her of a condition she remembers from her Liberal Ed psych class. Broca's aphasia they called it: *S. spoke, when she spoke at all, in a characteristic telegraphic manner, as though the words remained trapped inside the brain while only a few squeezed through.*

Giving up hope of conversation, Meredith pulls close the stack of books she had this morning borrowed from the library. She proceeds to entertain herself with selected morsels of fact and speculation.

6. AND THE SERPENT BITES ITS TAIL

Yehudi ("The Jew") Menuhin observed that "music, like language, has developed its own structures, grammars and vocabularies." Such words as "octave" and "fifth" are only convenient Western labels. For exam-

ple, the distance between any five steps in the scale is not always a perfect fifth. A series of fifths in a row will produce twelve separate notes before the notes begin repeating. This series of twelve notes, known as the circle of fifths, includes all the semitones of the Western scale. The piano keyboard is just wide enough to play the circle. If you start at the bottom, you will find that the thirteenth note at the top, seven octaves higher, is the same as the one on which you started.

C   C   F   B♭   G   E♭   D   A♭   A   C♯   E   B   F♯

"As it was in the beginning," Meredith declaims, "is now and ever shall be. World without end. Amen."

"Why do you always bring religion into it?" Sylvie says.

O god, if there is a god, give me wisdom, if there is such a thing as wisdom. To Sylvie she says, "I read something interesting about Yehudi Menuhin. When he was about ten, his younger sister Hepzibah cut off her hair. A bob. Their parents were very conservative. To punish her, they shaved her head. Yehudi was already famous then. He had a concert that night, but he shaved his own head. In sympathy."

"What's your point?" Sylvie says.

"No point," Meredith says. "It's just a nice story." But what Meredith thinks of, looking at Sylvie's closed-off face, is the quantum principle. *John Wheeler has said about the quantum principle: That it destroys the concept of the world as "sitting out there." Even to observe so minuscule an object as an electron, the observer must*

*reach in, must become a participator. The world will never afterwards
be the same.*

What, Meredith wants to ask, what if the world does not
want to let you in?

Mmmmnnnnnneeeaaah.

Bill's son talks. She's seen him. Of course *his* divorce
happened when the boy was just a preschooler. Teenagers take it
the worst.

*If your teenager exhibits any of the following behaviors, please call
TUFF-LUV:*

- *stays in his room a lot*
- *wears dark glasses*
- *becomes uncommunicative*

When Meredith was young there were fewer things to worry
about:

Punctuate fun fun fun worry worry worry

Fun period fun period fun no period worry worry worry

God, she thinks, Sylvie's just a baby herself. Her gaze shifts
to her daughter's waistline.

"Why are you looking at me?"

"Let's go out to dinner tonight. And maybe we'll stop at the
planetarium afterwards."

"The plane-TA-rium?!" Sylvie says. "MO-THER."

"It's next to that place you said you wanted to go to. Where
they shoot the food in your plate with the knife blade."

"I was going to go there with Dave," Sylvie says.

"There's a show at the planetarium," Meredith says. "It's

called the *Lumen and Decibel Show*. I heard about it from this guy at work. He's doing one of the demonstrations."

"Go with him then."

"I want to go with you."

"How long will it take?"

While Meredith is still calculating how many hours she will get away with, Sylvie says, "Okay."

It's just a quantum particle flying through.

7. SCHRÖDINGER'S CAT

The weirdness of the quantum world is not perceptible on the human scale. Except in the case of soft errors. To illustrate this weirdness, Erwin Schrödinger devised this thought experiment:

A kitten is placed in a closed box with a jar of poison and a triphammer poised to smash the jar. The hammer is activated by a switch that can be triggered by a random event of radioactive decay.

Schrödinger's cat in a superposition of eigenstates.

The experiment lasts just long enough so that a probability of fifty percent exists that the hammer will be released. A quantum mechanical view of the experiment is that the cat is fifty percent dead and fifty percent alive after the elapsed time. The question is whether the act of looking—the measurement—kills or saves the cat. Up until the moment of looking, the cat is said to be in a superposition of eigenstates.

They go to the restaurant in silence.

"Gross," Sylvie would say if Meredith were to tell her about Schrödinger's cat. "Why does it have to be something that kills the cat? Why don't they make it so the cat gets food or something?" But Meredith is not talking to Sylvie about quantum mechanics. She's not talking to her at all. She's holding out her bowl so that the chef can flip another shrimp into it.

Despite the informal atmosphere created by flying crustaceans, Sylvie is not spilling her guts. She's not even making small talk. She's eating. But eating is good. We are having fun, Meredith thinks.

At the planetarium exhibit they sit on opposite sides of a glass panel with lights on either side. The lights can be brightened or dimmed so that the barrier between mother and daughter traverses all the possibilities between opacity and transparency. *For now we see through a glass darkly.* In a fit of cooperation they follow the instructions and gradually adjust the light intensities in order to create an image on the screen consisting of a blend of their features. Meredith sees herself grow younger—years peeled away at the synchronized turn of two buttons—until it is no longer she on the screen, but a mixture of traces of herself and Sylvie. Cat/kitten, dead/alive.

From behind, Bill speaks into Meredith's hair. "So you came to be illuminated," he says. His hands are resting on her shoulders. His voice has a resonance that reminds her of the salty rumble of the ocean. She had noticed before, when he was near, the restless sloshing of primeval fluids under her skin. A full moon rises rib by rib in the firmament of her chest, and by its silver light kittenish tongues lap on the shore of his body attained.

"This is Sylvie," Meredith says. "My daughter."

"When you're done here come to my display," Bill says. He points. "Over there. I've set the *Jabberwocky* to music. With banjo strings and wine bottles. It's actually a re-creation of Pythagoras' harmonic ratios."

"You'll want to see that, Sylvie," Meredith says. To Bill: "She's making a soundscape for school."

"It's a dumb old school project," Sylvie says. She turns the switch on her side of the screen all the way down. Darkness collapses the wave function. When Meredith turns her head from Bill toward Sylvie, there is only one image in the mirror: the face of a woman, middle-aged. All that's visible of Sylvie is her back as she pushes through the crowd toward the door. Then she's gone.

"She's upset," Meredith says to Bill. "She broke up with her boyfriend."

"She'll want you, then," Bill says. "I'm sorry."

He's sorry—what? Meredith asks herself on her way to the

car. That two kids he doesn't know have broken up? Or that she needs me and he can't show me his banjo strings? Well, I'm sorry too. And I don't know what to do. This quality time thing is not working. It feels like doing time.

8. Pythagoras' comma

Lewis Carroll originally intended to print the entire Jabberwocky *in reversed form, but later decided to limit this to the first verse. The fact that the printing appeared reversed to Alice, is evidence that she herself was not reversed by her passage through the mirror. There are now scientific reasons for suspecting that an unreversed Alice could not exist for more than a fraction of a second in a looking-glass world.*

> **JABBERWOCKY**
>
> 'Twas brillig, and the slithy toves
> Did gyre and gimble in the wabe:
> All mimsy were the borogoves,
> And the mome raths outgrabe.

Sylvie is in the car, curled up on the backseat. "Pussycat," Meredith says through the rolled-down window. "You can't just run away from things."

"I'm not," Sylvie says. "I'm facing it." She is clutching a wallet-sized photograph to her chest. Tears drop from her cheeks onto its back. They turn the red felt-tip inscription into rivulets of blood.

Meredith gets in the back beside her. She finds a tissue in her purse, blots the back of the picture. "You're ruining it," she says.

"I don't care," Sylvie says. She sits up, turns the picture face up. "I hate him." She takes a pen from the seat pocket in front of her and starts blacking out his eyes. She has to do it with her left hand, because of the splint on her right one. Nevertheless, she perseveres until there are holes right through. Then she tears the picture in half, and starts tearing the mouth end in shreds.

When Meredith can no longer bear to just watch the slow-motion assault, she reaches for the other half of the picture and starts ripping. "Tear him to atoms," she says.

Beware the Jabberwock, my child!

"Thingamajigs," Sylvie says. "Split him."

The jaws that bite, the claws that catch!

"Quarks," Meredith says. "That's as small as it gets."

Beware the Jujub bird, and shun

The frumious Bandersnatch!

"The wind will blow him into the desert."

"Cosmic rays will push him around."

"He's going with Maren," Sylvie says. "I hate her too."

Meredith offers to drive out of the city so that Sylvie can release pinches of Dave to the wind.

"I don't even *like* Brad. I was trying to get him to ask Kirstin to the prom."

When the sun is almost down, mother and daughter end up at the lake. They stay parked on the shore until the angry red above the water fades to pink. The sinuous trail of a jet diving into the sunset divides the sky into the complementary halves of the *t'ai-chi* symbol. Yin, Yang. *Can't have one without the other.*

Meredith, as usual, takes direction from the wisdom of the ancients. "When Pythagoras invented the math for the harmonic ratios, he discovered that every now and then the math way would sound wrong. The formula had to be adjusted every few notes to make the notes compatible with our ears. But Pythagoras never let on that the math way was wrong. He kept it a secret, because he believed that numbers made a circle in the mind of God, and that the circle had to be perfect. When musicians found this out, they called the difference between the math way and the listening way *Pythagoras' comma.*"

Other sages have a word:

Einstein: As far as the laws of mathematics refer to reality, they are not certain; as far as they are certain, they do not refer to reality.

Chuan Tzu: If it could be talked about, everybody would have told their brother.

Sylvie: Every object makes a sound if only the right thing strikes it.

Meredith carries an open wine bottle and a glass into the living room. The chair across from her is empty. If Bill were there, she would tell him the words she knows that end in -th. *Coolth.* When she was a child in South Africa and complained about the heat, her mother used to say, *Go lie down in the coolth under your bed.* She often took her mother's advice, taking along the dictionary to while away the time. *Plinth, shibboleth. Azimuth, zenith.* The word *musth* was not in that dictionary, she believes. She first heard this word after moving to America. It was on PBS. She thought the announcer was talking about the Iditarod and had a speech impediment. Just this morning she heard another word that at first confused her. Moshing. It refers to a new kind of dancing. A bunch of teenagers hold onto someone's arms and twirl him around until he soars above the ground. Then they let go, and he smashes into a pile of fellow-dancers. She wonders if Bill knows this. In the morning she might call him and bring it up. She reaches behind her to her desk and picks up yesterday's computer printout. There is nothing on it that makes sense. Her thoughts drift away. *Moshing.* It's something parents should know about. It can paralyze a teenager.

Meredith pours herself some wine. When she puts the bottle down, a few drops dribble down from the lip and spread around the base to form a circle on the printout it rests on, a circle Meredith would see when she next set the bottle down after topping up her glass. By then it would be half empty, so that, if one were to tap its side with a spoon, the glass would sound a tone somewhere in the middle of the circle of harmony in Pythagoras' mind. For now the only sounds are Sylvie's.

When they got home Sylvie returned to her project. Her sounds drift over from the kitchen, fill the space above the meniscus in the wine bottle. A gonglike sound reverberates, followed by a scraping that ends the cycle, gentle as an afterthought. A succession of compressions and rarefactions carries Sylvie's sounds through the spheres, past the outermost one, where, for all Meredith knows, they simply disappear. Or where, she thinks with gratitude, their trill might stir an angel. *Those who have ears, let them hear.*

No Money for Stamps

FALL, 1984

Two years after they had moved to America, Magriet's husband Becker told her he'd had an affair. But it was over, done with, he said. He didn't know what had come over him. They were in the kitchen after dinner, Becker having lingered to help with the cleanup like he did on nights when he was planning sex. The children were upstairs. Becker, groping distractedly in the dirty dishwater as if searching for a utensil he might have missed, said, "Forgive me, Griet. Please."

Magriet thought of the pastor, Terence, who used to minister to her maid Rose in their backyard in South Africa. He had the forgiving mien of a TV evangelist. When he smiled, teeth of the kind that set cartoonists scrambling for their sketch pads started out of his mouth. Remembering their porcelain shine against his dark lips, Magriet burst out laughing.

Becker took the dishcloth from her and dried his hands like Pontius Pilate. "My Griet," he said, "I'm so sorry."

Magriet raised the platter she had just dried and hurled it to the floor. The only time she'd deliberately broken a plate before was at the bon voyage party their friends had given them when they'd emigrated. It had been a surprise, held at a Greek restaurant. The management supplied cheap crockery for breaking, dishes purposely underfired to keep them brittle. You could get them from your waiter in sets of a dozen. At the end of the night they were added to your check. Now Magriet banged around the kitchen looking for something else to throw.

Becker tracked her at a nervous distance like a boxer looking for an opening. "The kids," he said.

She whirled around and faced him. "You think hearing a plate break is going to hurt them?" She started to cry.

Becker reached for her, and she shielded herself as if to ward off a blow.

"Don't touch me," she said, "ever again."

When, after about two months, it appeared Magriet had meant what she'd said, Becker found himself a room to rent. He had gathered his clothes and stood in the bedroom doorway, a squalling child on each hip. "Magriet," he said, his face between their heads, "I cannot make it up to you if you're not there to be made up to."

It occurred to Magriet that without Becker in her life she would never hear her name properly pronounced. She stepped toward him and lifted first Kate, who was seven, and then Rian, four, from his arms. "You will see Daddy tomorrow," she said, taking each child by the hand. "Say good-bye now. We're going to get a video from the library. And we'll stop for ice cream." But they pulled away from her and clung to Becker's legs.

As Becker spoke softly to the kids and brought them over to her, she remembered something she'd read in a book he had given her long ago in South Africa. Chaos was good, the book said, it was the wellspring of novelty in the universe. It showed the laws of nature were not fixed, the past history of a system did not always determine its next instant. The future, rather, depended very sensitively on incredibly minute changes in particular conditions. The book had given the hypothetical example that the flap of a butterfly's wings in Brazil could set off a tornado in Texas.

The next day Magriet spoke to her friend Shauna's husband, a lawyer, about getting a divorce. Afterwards she knew in her gut what she had only known rationally before: her fate was tied to Becker's. Her staying in America was predicated on the fact that she was Becker's wife. She was not allowed to work in the United States until they had qualified for a green card, and Becker, because he had the work permit and the job, was the only one of them eligible to apply. Magriet's anger at Becker about this state of affairs blended into an old, familiar discontent, so that when he came by to pick up the kids that night, she could barely manage the most basic civility. And later, on days he dropped off a check, she found it necessary to be in the bathroom or on the phone so she would not have to take money from his hand.

After Becker had been away some weeks, Magriet decided—

work permit or not—she had to get a job. She asked her friend Shauna whether the opening in her gift shop had been filled. Shauna said no and, after cautioning Magriet not to mention it to her lawyer husband, offered her the position. "Your English is so cultured," she said, "no one would think to check your papers." Magriet was ecstatic until she discovered her pay would be less than it would cost to put Rian in day care. It was then that she started scanning the help wanted ads in the paper. One caught her eye. "Nanny for darling three-year-old boy. Light house-keeping." She called, explained that she was a single mother with an extraordinarily well-behaved four-year-old, and got the job.

The child she took care of was shy, mild-tempered, and most of the time willing to share his toys with Rian. The family dog was hyperactive and barked constantly. The pay and the hours were good. Her employer was a divorcee with no apparent job, and with an unexplained access to wealth. She would wait until Magriet arrived each morning, set out for the day without saying where she was going, and return promptly when it was time for Magriet to pick Kate up from school.

Magriet felt lucky. She buckled down, dealt daily with other people's dinner dishes on which the night before's food had hardened, shook out satin sheets bristling with dog hairs, fed the dog an unauthorized half a Valium in its breakfast every morning, and, when her chores were done, read the boys stories and taught them the binomial theorem with building blocks.

In what seemed to have been a different incarnation, Magriet had taught math at the University of Pretoria. She had Becker to thank that she'd persisted with a graduate degree in math. Becker had convinced her of how smart she was. She'd met Becker when she was an undergrad and he a teaching assistant. They'd immediately fallen in love. Becker, who was married at the time—"a youthful mistake"—got divorced. They'd moved in together. "We don't need a piece of paper to prove our commitment," Becker had assured her. Magriet had wholeheartedly agreed, ready as she'd been to follow Becker to the ends of the earth. Magriet's father had had a different perspective. Not a particularly religious man, when confronted with a daughter living in sin he'd become fanatical in his own secular way. "You cannot ignore the rituals of the civilized world," he'd told her. "That's all that stands between us and them."

Becker's comment after the children had told him about Magriet's job reminded her of her father. "What the fuck," Becker said. "You're white."

MAY, 1981

Rose came with the house. Like the pool.

Becker was the one who wanted the pool. In fact, the whole thing was Becker's idea: getting out of the country before the blacks took over. With the exchange rate so bad, that was going to take a lot of money. So, although Magriet was almost eight months pregnant with Rian, they put their newly renovated house on the market. When they received an offer within the month, they went looking for something cheap to rent. In the older part of their neighborhood they stopped at a ramshackle house with a "To Let" sign on the front gate. A woman appeared from the servant's room and offered to show them around. Inside, the potential of pressed steel ceilings and wood floors somewhat lifted Magriet's spirits, but by the time they reached the back door she had remembered that in this house nothing would be fixed, that she would have to remember not to love it too much, like a foster child.

Their guide led them up the steps to the garden. "The pool," she said with the suppressed pride of someone lifting the lid off a casserole.

Becker was immediately enthusiastic. "I'm going to teach Kate to swim," he said. "I used to be on the swim team."

"The pool is green," Magriet said. "Kate is only four."

But she could see from Becker's measuring glance in the direction of the algae-infested water that he was already seeing a clear blue rectangle, bisected by a white wake foaming behind Kate's kicking feet. "In America," he said, "we won't have a pool. We'll be the poor whites."

Magriet nodded meaningfully in the direction of the woman who was accompanying them and tried to catch Becker's eye. She thought the way Becker spoke about poor whites in front of a black woman was inappropriate. Becker always did that. Acted as if servants were part of the scenery. When she'd confronted him about it early in their relationship, he'd accused her of being a bleeding heart. "The only reason they are in company is because they are servants. They are there to do a job, and the conversation has nothing to do with them. It has nothing to do with the fact that they're black." Magriet had violently disagreed. Although she'd quoted Kant's categorical imperative at him, Becker had not changed his behavior. "I say it as I see it," Becker always said, and she had to grant him: he was just as likely to be rude to white people. Now she shrugged her embarrassment away and turned to the woman to ask her name. "My name is Rose," the woman said.

To Becker Magriet said, "It's dirty. The fence is broken." She pointed to a gap big enough for a car to drive through, where three of four sections of the wooden enclosure had collapsed into the adjacent flower bed. "Kate is going to drown. I won't have time to watch her when the baby's here."

Rose spoke from behind them. "I am going to watch your girl," she said. "And the boy." She patted Magriet's stomach. "The master he going to fix the fence."

"We don't know what the baby is," Magriet said. "I told the doctor not to tell me."

"Yes," Becker said. "The old girl is right. I'm going to fix it."

"It's a boy," Rose said. "You carrying wide."

She was right about the baby's sex. Their son was born in the week between their looking at the house and moving in. When they arrived at the gate with the new baby, and with their possessions piled onto a borrowed truck, Rose was there, immaculate in her starched apron and cap, having apparently taken their earlier interaction as a job contract. She met them with a proprietary welcome. Magriet found herself apologizing that their best things were already in boxes for America, and that the scraggly items they were unloading were soon to be discarded. Rose said she would organize a jumble sale at the end of their stay. She took the baby from Magriet's arms, exclaimed that she had never seen such a strong-looking boy. She crooned and chatted. She called him her Punzi. She handed him back, and turned to take charge of the melee of unloading and unpacking. So capable did she seem that Magriet left the decisions to her and Becker and betook herself and the baby to the backyard, where she lay on a blanket watching Kate to ensure she would not drown.

"The old ones are better," Becker had said that night.

Rose appeared about fifty. "It will be like having my mother live in," Magriet said.

"At least we won't have boyfriend problems. And I checked her pass. She's stamped to work in Johannesburg."

So Rose was there from the beginning of the end, when Magriet was already storing up memories to be looked back upon later.

WINTER, 1984

After an interval that seemed much longer than the month it was, Magriet had a day off. She walked Kate to school, had a snowball fight with Rian, and returned home to confront her own home's mess. The previous night's dinner plates were interspersed with that morning's cereal bowls. Kate's Thanksgiving project, a dismemberment of turkeys and pilgrims, was spread out on the floor.

Magriet longed for Rose. She admitted it was because Rose

had been good at whipping domestic chaos into order. But it was also because early morning used to be Rose's designated slot for talking from the heart. So, instead of stacking the plates in the sink and running water over them so the spaghetti sauce and chocolate flakes could soak, she cleared a place for herself next to Rian on the couch and succumbed to the cartoons. As the speech impediments of animated characters gave way to the loquacious-ness of talk show guests, Rian drifted away in play, but Magriet stayed. She marveled at how Americans could come clean, could hug and cry and tell each other "I love you" in public. She imag-ined herself on the TV stage. To spare the host the trouble of her unsayable name, she would tell him, "Just call me Margaret." Then she would start talking. After a while the host would lean sympathetically toward her, offering a box of tissues.

JUNE, 1981

Because she now had Rose, Magriet resumed the math tutoring she had given up because of the baby. Mondays through Thurs-days she prepared lessons after lunch for the Standard Nine pupils who arrived as soon as school was out. She felt lucky to be keep-ing some part of her brain alive. That day, because the weather was so warm for winter, she sat outside on a garden chair. The baby lay on a towel beside her. Kate, four years old, was tossing a stuffed frog to and fro. She was wearing her princess dress, the silver mini Magriet had in a previous life worn to her Matric dance. Kate was supposed to play where Rose could see her, because Becker had not yet fixed the fence, but she kept wandering back to her mother.

Magriet worried she was not giving Kate enough attention. She wanted to be a good mother, like the woman on TV who taught her children the alphabet before they were two.

Rose's initial display of public relations did not last. Silent and dour that day, she swayed up the garden steps with a tub of laundry balanced on her head. Light flickered across her face when she saw the baby: her Punzi. Her eyes fell on Kate, who was picking up leaves from the lawn and throwing them onto the green scum coating the pool.

"Once upon a time," Kate said, "there was a princess. And then her golden ball fell in the pool."

"You must not play with dirt, Mizkatie," Rose said. "Play with your toys. You making a mess."

The things they latch on to, Magriet thought. *Their own children have nothing but sticks and rocks to play with.* She sighed. "Oh, Rose. Nothing Kate does can make the pool any worse. I promised the master I'd put in the chemicals, but I only have half an hour to prepare and my students will be here."

"The master must fix the pool," Rose said. "That dirty job will take your milk away, Ma'am."

Magriet smiled. She did not believe the old wives' tale of milk drying up, but she did not want to argue with Rose. She felt she had an ally in her. A woman who sympathized with her. Lately she'd been feeling overburdened and misunderstood. She thought Becker did not appreciate the pressures on her. He was a good husband and made enough money for both of them. For all of them. Enough to put away for America, and to still employ a maid who cleaned the house and did the diapers. Magriet knew she was lucky and shouldn't be tired. For the last two weeks, though, she hadn't been able to go back to sleep after the baby's midnight feeding. She had taken to getting up and reading instead of lying awake. At the moment she was intrigued with a book Becker had given her, called *Chaos and Order.* At first glance she thought it was about the political situation in the country, but when she looked closer she realized it dealt with the new theory Prigogine had gotten the Nobel Prize for. Pleased that Becker hadn't forgotten she used to be a mathematician, she started the book, and could not stop. She still could not put it down once she took it up. It described a scientific attempt to deal with systems so complex that their details and motions were beyond description in linear mathematics. Prigogine's ideas excited her. *Only dead things can truly be in equilibrium. The price of being alive is not to be in equilibrium.* It seemed to her these scientific insights had something to do with her life, that if only she could concentrate long enough to fully understand them, she would be able to arrange her life to work better. Because everything seemed out of control. By midday she saw the world through a grey and gritty fog, and could concentrate on nothing more than figuring the hours before she could go to sleep again.

"Then have an afternoon nap," Becker said when he realized how exhausted she was. "That's why I got you a servant."

"You got me a servant?" Magriet said. "Excuse me. Rose appointed herself."

"But I'm paying her," Becker said. Which he shouldn't have.

Magriet was holding it against him that her tiredness had only become apparent to him now, when, for the nth time in a row, she'd been too tired for sex. "You stay home with the baby and I'll go back to work," she said. The next day she made arrangements to resume her tutoring. Becker was smart enough not to say anything, but she knew what he was thinking: what she would earn was not worth the trouble, that she should rather take a nap. That was probably true. But tutoring made her feel like a person. At the time of Kate's birth she had given up her university teaching job because she wanted to be a full-time mother. Now she felt as if becoming a parent had turned her into a nonentity, while Becker's life was going on pretty much as before. It was *her* brain that was atrophying. It seemed her teaching in the afternoons was all that stood between her and the flat line of brain death. But now, while in a garden chair preparing for the day's lesson, she had to admit Becker was right about the nap. She needed one. And her body was taking one without her permission. Her copy of *A New Senior Mathematics* kept slipping from her lap.

Magriet hitched the book back into focus and found the theorem she was going to explain to her students. She stared at the diagram. A parallelogram shifted into two duplicates of itself that lifted off the page. The sigh of her breath billowed their shapes into the sails of a tall ship. Her father was standing on deck. He pointed at the sails. "A quadrilateral with its opposite sides parallel," she said. Her father laughed. "This isn't geometry," he said. "This is history." Magriet noticed they were on the beach in Table Bay. The sails belonged to Jan van Riebeeck's three ships, aground in the shallows behind the surf. "He should have sailed on," her father said. "He should have left Africa undiscovered, so the kaffirs could finish each other off."

The loose swing of Magriet's head onto her chest tore a ragged black strip through the scene. When she opened her eyes, Rose's apron was what she saw. "Ma'am," Rose said. "Your students are here."

DECEMBER, 1984

When Magriet asked the children what they wanted for Christmas, they both said, *Daddy.* She was unable to say no. When she told Shauna what she had consented to, her friend brought out the Christmas present she had been planning to give her, and told her to open it right away. It was a relationship self-help book, *How to Find the Love You Deserve.* "Becker is a good man," Shauna said. "You just have to figure out how to work him."

Deserve? Magriet thought. *That's what I'm afraid of.*

JUNE, 1981

Over the math books strewn on the dining room table a child's voice insinuated itself among the converging lines of an insight Magriet was about to convey to her students.

"Mama, Rose won't fetch Stradivarius for me," Kate said.

"You mustn't order Rose around. Fetch him yourself, then you go play. Mama's busy."

"But he doesn't know how to swim and he's getting all wet."

"Oh my god, the pool," Magriet cried. She ran to the back

door. "Where's Rose?" she asked Kate. "She's supposed to look after you."

"She's gone to get Beauty," Kate said.

"Who's Beauty?" Magriet asked.

Kate did not answer. She was wobbling around the corner on her bike. Magriet followed. She was furious at Rose for having let Kate out of her sight, and was getting a lecture ready in her head. But when she reached the gate, Rose had unlocked it and was showing off the sleeping baby on her back to a young woman she had let in. When she saw Magriet, Rose proudly introduced the newcomer as her daughter, Beauty. The daughter—a mere girl, Magriet saw—giggled behind her hand. Beauty was on vacation from the teachers' training college, Rose said, and was going to take care of Kate and the Punzi so Rose could get on with the scrubbing and ironing.

Magriet's first thought was that she might as well use the extra help. She was starting to feel like Becker's mother, who had so many servants she spoke about "the staff." She shook Beauty's hand. "Pleased to meet you, Beauty," she said. To Rose, she said, "You did not tell me your daughter was coming."

"Beauty and the Beast," Kate said.

"You busy with the children, Ma'am."

"Yes, I'm busy, Rose," Magriet said. "Kate was playing by the pool. You have to look after her. I can't do my work."

"Mizkatie," Rose said. "You must stay by me. God will punish you."

Magriet did not want Rose to threaten Kate with God, but she did not know how to tell her not to.

"Beauty is Beauty," Kate said, "and Rose is the Beast." Kate laughed at her joke and danced for attention. "Rose is Rose Red and Beauty is Snow White."

Beauty said something for the first time. She looked right into Magriet's face. "Those Grimm stories are bad for the children," she said. "They telling us so by the Teachers' Training."

Magriet first heard "grim," and then adjusted to "Grimm," which, she supposed, amounted to the same thing. She was taken aback. Her child rearing was being questioned. She didn't know what to say to Beauty, so she turned to Rose. "Rose," she said, "those students are paying me to teach them geometry and I'm paying you to watch the children. And get Kate's frog out of the pool." *Magriet is the witch*, she thought.

Beauty spoke to Kate. "Beauty is not Snow White," she said. She knelt in front of Kate and took her hands in hers. She cupped them around her face, held them down with hers. "Beauty is black."

"Black Beauty," Kate said.

"Yes," Beauty said. "Black is beautiful." She got up and took Kate's hand. She skipped with her to the pool. Magriet waited in the door until Rose had fished out the frog and moved away from the pool. Leaving behind Rose, who stopped every few steps to squeeze water out of the toy, Beauty and Kate cantered ahead.

Magriet felt her life was too complicated after Beauty's arrival. One afternoon Beauty did her own laundry and hung her dresses and underwear out over the pool fence to dry. The high school boys coming for math lessons pointed at the bras and panties and told jokes behind their hands that Magriet did not even want to imagine. Magriet felt if she now told Beauty to take her under-wear away, it would just make things worse. So she left it. But before Becker got home, she told her to gather up her stuff. He would have thrown a fit. "We're not even gone and they're taking over already," he would have said.

He did not want Beauty to be there at all. So Magriet had to make sure she was invisible. When Rose had sent Beauty in with his coffee and introduced her the first night, Becker had said, "What about her pass?"

"I will hide her, Master," Rose had said. "She pass is not right for Johburg."

Magriet had been relieved there was a legal reason for Beauty not to be here. Beauty's critique of fairy tales had unnerved her. "That's ridiculous, Rose," she'd said. "You cannot hide her for—how long is she here for?"

"Two months, Ma'am," Rose had said. She'd cited the prece-dent of many years with her previous employer. Beauty would be safe from pass inspectors as long as she stayed inside the locked gates. Then, if someone in the dreaded khaki uniform rang the bell, there would be plenty of time for Beauty to hide under Rose's bed. "She going to be fine."

Magriet had been ready to reply with a rational argument that one could not expect a young woman to stay behind locked gates for a month, and that it would be better for Beauty to go somewhere where she would have more freedom, when Becker had said—or rather—Becker had shouted, "She's not going to be fine. She's going to be *fined!* And who is going to have to pay that fine? Me."

Magriet had been raised not to argue in front of the servants, but she was so angry at Becker's reminder that she was not earning any meaningful money, she forgot where she was. "Why is money always the issue?" she'd asked. She was shouting too. "Don't you think other things are important too? Like a mother being able to spend time with her daughter?"

Rose had made summoning motions with her hand to get Beauty out of the room, but Beauty had watched entranced.

"Let them go to their own place to spend time together," Becker had said. "Let them go somewhere where I won't be the one to pay."

Rose had tugged at Beauty to get her to leave, but Beauty had wiped her mother's hand away.

"I'm going to phone the pass office," Magriet had said. "There must be some way to get a temporary pass."

"If you touch that phone," Becker had said, "they'll be here before you even put it down. She's just going to have to go back."

"Go back where?" Magriet had asked. She'd thought of her own weekends at boarding school when everyone not living on a faraway farm used to go home and she used to be left alone with the two girls from the orphanage and the matron, who, it was rumored, walked in on the stay-behinds when they were in the bath and offered to wash their backs.

"That's not our problem," Becker had said. He'd gotten up from his chair and stomped out of the room. "Five hundred rand," he'd said.

"Ma'am," Beauty had said. "By the pass office you must call

me Ntsanwisi Mponyana. By the Teachers' Training, we voted we're not going by white names no more."

When Becker had left for work the next morning, Magriet had called the pass office and made carefully formulated general inquiries without mentioning names, white or other-hued. But in the end, as she'd had to tell Rose with embarrassment after putting the phone down, the only way Beauty could spend more than forty-eight hours with her mother was in their time-tested way of hiding her under the bed.

"And Rose," Magriet had said, not believing what was coming out of her mouth, "I am going to tell the master we got her a temporary pass. Else he is just going to worry."

"That okay, Ma'am," Rose had said.

Now that Beauty's stay had been secured, Rose decided to pass more of the child care on to her daughter so she herself could find piece jobs in the neighborhood to supplement what Becker paid her. The Teachers' Training was expensive, she said. And when Beauty's education had been taken care of, Rose was going to save for her to go to America. The unattainability of this ideal so took Magriet's breath away, she forgot to take it up with Rose that she'd rather not have Beauty in charge of the children. By the time she had built up courage to raise the issue, Rose forestalled her attempt with news of a lucrative job she'd landed just down the road.

Rose found jobs easily, but she did not keep them. Her moral standards prevented her from working for people who didn't live right, she told Magriet. "Those Italians, Ma'am. They let the dog sleep in the bed." Magriet herself recommended the couple across the road, a balding fortyish man with two children and a new wife who looked barely twenty. Magriet could not have known the wife's deficiencies as a mother—she gave the children breakfast cereal at dinnertime—would make it impossible for Rose to do their ironing.

Rose's moral code derived from her membership in the Nazareth Baptist Church of Sheme. Armored against sin in her matron's uniform of yellow poplin she set out on Sundays for all-day meetings in a neighbor's garage. On weekdays her beliefs were evinced in apocalyptic pronouncements over the breakfast dishes, or, occasionally, by the visitation of evil spirits whose exorcism required hours of prayer in a darkened room.

Rose's pastor was a regular at the gate, dropping in at least once a week on his round of home visits. The first time he came to minister Rose brought him to the back door to meet Magriet. Terence was his name. After lifting a hand in blessing on Kate and the baby, he sat down with Rose in the courtyard on chairs she borrowed from the kitchen for the occasion. Some days, by evening, all the kitchen chairs were outside. Rose had many visitors. Cousins, aunts, and the children of friends began to ring the bell at all hours.

In the middle of the night, three months after moving into the house with the pool, there sat Magriet: thirty-three, mother of two, mistress of a household. She was rocking the baby. A stretch of her leg away lay Becker, diagonally across the bed. She touched her toe to his foot poking through the sheets. His snoring stopped abruptly and he patted her side of the bed with the flat of his hand before sinking back into his dream.

"It's just you and me," Magriet said into the down of her son's head. "Just me and my little piggy." She wondered what the teachers' college's take was on nursery rhymes. *The little piggy who went to market.* Becker said when they took over there would be no market—this was his punch line—except for the black market. She did not want to think about these things now. She moved her lips across the bony hardness of the baby's skull. She touched her tongue to that thin barrier between his wordless brain and the world. With her forefinger she shaped the scraggly hair on his forehead into an upside down question mark. His grunts rose in foamy peaks on the purl of faraway traffic.

She followed the easy ins and outs of her own breath, and soon came that wavy world where the honk of a horn yielded a baby, dressed for a great occasion. A christening? No, she and Becker (who was there, suddenly, in the way of dreams) would not lay *that* burden on their children. A wedding? Yes. The bride, who had grown to full size, turned, and then it was Magriet who was behind the veil, and the lacy fabric a great weight when she tried to lift it. The lace split in half and a chasm opened up into which the baby dropped. As she thrust both hands in after him, she woke up. The baby wailed. Her grasp on his arm had pulled him from her breast. Fear sliced cold through her heart as she lifted him to her shoulder.

CHRISTMAS EVE, 1984

Through the children's initiative, Magriet's concession that Becker could spend Christmas Day with them had evolved into a sleep-over. On Christmas Eve around ten P.M., he was asleep with both children in what used to be his and Magriet's bed. Kate had asked Magriet to sleep there too, but she had declined. Exhausted after having nannied all day while her employer did her last-minute shopping, she had gone off by herself to the children's room and had fallen asleep in Kate's bed. After an indefinable time period, the icy laser of a nightmare stung her awake. An unnamable dread left her too scared to move. She knew she was in bed, but had no sense of her location in time or the world. As she waited out the damping of her heart's runaway rhythm, images of places where she had regularly woken up during other phases of her life played on the dark screen behind her eyelids: a rectangle of star-spangled sky from her African farm childhood; the parallel slats of her own babies' cribs as she had awakened in their rooms after dozing off in the rocking chair during the two A.M. feeding; the shivering fractals of pool-reflected city lights on squares of pressed steel. As one by one she rejected these anchors to security, she heard her mother's voice behind the drumming that reverberated in her head. *Feel.* She walked the fingers of her right hand away from her body in tiny steps. The emptiness beside her reminded her where she was.

The knowledge of her whereabouts gave her no relief. Keeping her eyes scrunched closed, she thought back to an incident that had happened when she was seven. They lived on the farm then. The maid, who at that time worked in the house, was Sarah. In winter, six of her children died. The only one left was the baby. Before, and for a while after, Sarah used to bring him to work with her, laying him on a gunnysack by the back door, or strapping him to her back while she ironed or polished the floor. When they were still alive, the other children lived on the other side of the dam in a shack with rocks to hold the roof down and a black round-bellied pot on the ground in front of it. Magriet and her brothers were not allowed to go there, because those people were not clean, but they sometimes watched from the bullrushes on the dam wall how Sarah's kids built a snare with the lid of the round-bellied pot and a lure of cornmeal mush to trap red and yellow kafferfinks. When the row of plucked birds laid out on the dirt added up to maybe a dozen, they would take them to the tobacco barn and cook them in one of the drying ovens. They ate them hot off the fire, tossing the charred lumps from hand to hand until they'd cooled enough to pull off the head and feet. Magriet could see what they did was unhygienic. She was not surprised when Sarah said one day that there was illness at her house.

Some days later Magriet and her brothers and sister were on the living room carpet under the blanket named "Wollie" for a bedtime story when her father came in and whispered in her mother's ear. Then he went to his chair to listen to the radio. Magriet's mother finished reading, and sat quietly for a while. "You have to make your own beds tomorrow," she said. "Sarah won't be in."

It was not that Magriet even knew these children's names, but later in the bedroom she shared with baby Bella, when a night terror thrust her into a frozen wakefulness, she knew Sarah's dead children were the reason she was too petrified to move. Maybe not knowing their names was why her unconscious had to substitute for the six dead children in her dream two each of her brothers Pieter and Johan, and two of her baby sister, Bella. The thought that if Sarah's baby had also died Magriet herself might have had to take a place in the lineup of dead children, was what had driven her from her bed to the living room, where the radio was just then beeping to announce the late news.

Her mother was up, but she had Bella on her lap. So it was her father who motioned for her to come to his chair. He scooped her into his lap. "Listen," he said. His breath was edged with the same smell that permeated the tobacco barns. "This is history. It's Harold MacMillan. He talked at Parliament today." *Winds of change*, the sonorous British voice on the radio said, *winds of change are sweeping this continent.*

"Bloody Soutie," her father said when it was over. "What does he know about what's good for this country?" He touched Magriet's elbow and she slid off his knees. He walked outside to look for Sputnik. Often when she had nightmares he took her outside to show her the Southern Cross. "Don't confuse it with the False Cross," he would caution. But that night he left her inside.

"Come here," her mother said. When Magriet stepped closer, hesitantly, because there was something unknown in her mother's voice, her mother took her hand and placed it on the baby's head. "Feel," she said. Something warm pulsated there, alive and frightened like a swallow that had flown in through a window and exhausted itself in trying to find the way out so you could pick it up and feel its heart in your hand before you thrust it out the door toward the open sky.

"Feel," Magriet's mother said again. She put her hand on Magriet's and worked it over the sleeping Bella's hair as if her hand were the soft pink baby brush with the picture of the rabbit on the handle. Then she said, "You must not trouble yourself about Sarah's children. Those people don't feel about their children the way we do."

Mother, Mother, tell me true, Magriet now thought, although her mother had died when Magriet was pregnant with Kate. And Kate was already as old as Magriet was when the nameless children had died. But, of course, her mother turned out to have been right. Not long after, Sarah sent the alive baby away. To live with its grandmother on another farm. Magriet was there when her mother asked Sarah why. "He getting too heavy," Sarah said. Then, although Magriet was seven already, her mother picked her up and put her on her hip as if she were Bella, and carried her out of the room.

While Magriet was remembering this incident, she became aware of opening and closing sounds from below. She opened her eyes. A lozenge of blue light shone in the dark: it was the TV screen in the living room downstairs, reflected in the mirror. It had to be Becker prowling about, probably microwaving some popcorn, as he did when he could not sleep.

She got up and went down to the kitchen. Becker, as she had imagined, was there. He offered to make her some tea. She accepted, then sat in the living room watching TV while he boiled the water. After he'd brought her the tea, he sat down next to her and said, out of the blue, "Remember when we went to see the moon landing at the Pigalle?"

Magriet did not know what to make of his reminiscence. The moon landing was the day they counted their relationship from. She sipped her tea. "Yes," she said. "I remember. The deaf school's children were there, talking with their hands."

"I never thought it was strange, then," Becker said, "that there was no TV in South Africa. Whenever something happened in the world we had to wait until it got to the newsreel at the movies."

"We got TV when I was pregnant with Kate," she said.

"You were watching Princess Di walk up the aisle when your water broke. I couldn't get you to go to the hospital until I'd promised to tape the wedding."

She laughed. It was one of their family legends. She'd refused to get in the car until he'd set up the VCR. After Kate had been born and she'd returned home, she'd viewed the end of the event on tape. When Kate was a toddler, the Royal Wedding was as familiar to her as Disney's *Sleeping Beauty*.

Magriet's thoughts followed a chain of associations that brought her back to Rose. She remembered a day when Kate and Beauty had watched the wedding tape. But she did not reminisce about it with Becker. Instead she finished her tea, said good night, and went back to bed.

The next morning, in addition to a number of extravagant

surprises for the children, there was a mystery package under the tree. It was for Magriet from Becker. A computer. It came with an accounting program so that, he explained, she would not have to work for that woman anymore. She could make money from home by doing small businesses' books. A woman who now worked at his company, also an immigrant, had put two kids through college doing that.

Magriet watched as Becker set up the computer and loaded her program and some games for the children. He also installed a screen saver. When he was done, he called her over to see: a squat, expanding, wart-covered snowman zoomed toward her, its inside exploding into a riot of tendrils and curlicues as it grew. Once, long ago, she had known the math behind the patterns on the screen, but now her knowledge had shrunk to what could be intimated by buzzwords that had suddenly become popular: fractals, the Mandelbrot set. As she stared at the ever repeating but always different organic-seeming contours of chaos, characters from her children's books, rather than equations, presented themselves to her: sea horses riding the jet streams of geometry, dragons clawing their own tails, rainbow-hued galaxies scattering vivid sparks.

Becker was reading to the children from the program booklet. "Fractal curves," he read, "can wiggle so much they fall in the gap between two dimensions."

The children were not interested. Rian wanted to play the game with the frogs again, and Kate was whiny and clingy in anticipation of the fact that Becker was about to go back to his own place.

JULY, 1981

Magriet was on the living room couch nursing the baby, and Rose was busying herself with nearby chores. Her dust rag lingered on the gilt that framed Becker and Magriet's stern young faces in the wedding portrait on the mantelpiece. "Beauty she must wear a white dress like so when she get married."

Magriet's thoughts flashed back to the night before. When she got back into bed after feeding the baby, Becker had turned on his side so his body made a template into which she fitted the curve of her back. His mouth made wet, chewing sounds and his hand groped for her breast. It felt flaccid and empty when he touched it. She mimicked sleep with the slow measure of her breath, but he pulled her thigh against his crotch. She drew away and said, "I've been up with the baby."

Becker had slid over to his side of the bed and gotten out. "I'm not stupid," he'd said. "You're doing it with someone else." And then he'd left the room and the house, and had not yet, at the time of Magriet's last phone call a few minutes before, shown up at his office.

"Beauty must look like this when she get married," Rose repeated.

Magriet wanted to tell Rose how mistaken one could be even in a white dress, but she didn't believe in discussing one's problems with servants. So she was condemned to small talk. "How about you, Rose?" she asked. "How did you get married?"

Rose's face sobered into guilt. "I got married the old way, Ma'am. No church, just lobola."

"What did your father ask for you, Rose?"

"Three cows, Ma'am. My family was high then. But now we have come low. But I can still work, Ma'am. Beauty she must marry by the way of the Lord like you, Ma'am." She handed Magriet the photograph of the bride that was she four and a half years ago. When Magriet did not comment, Rose continued. "America, she's got black people, Ma'am?" she asked.

While she looked at the picture, Magriet answered yes, and told about the preacher Martin Luther King Jr. He was killed sometime before she'd first met Becker, but that part she did not tell. Instead she quoted an uplifting line she remembered being cited during the radio reports of his death. "In America," she said, "little white girls and boys can play with little black girls and boys, and it is not against the law." But her mind was not on what she said. It was focused on the unrelenting blankness of her youthful face—an expression not softened by the lace and silk of the elaborate gown. When she'd called Becker from her parents' house on the night before the ceremony, he'd taken a long time picking up the phone. "I miss you," she'd said.

He was silent for a long time, as if figuring the answer to a difficult problem. A burst of background laughter almost erased his voice when he spoke. But through the noise she distinguished her name, the pronunciation altered to indicate possession, which had become his pet name for her. "My Griet."

She was supposed to respond, "Maar nie verniet," Afrikaans for *but not without cost*, but their lovers' game now made her gag. Instead, she stated the obvious. "You're having a party."

"I'm having a bachelor's party. Because I'm a bachelor." He laughed conspiratorially.

"You're drunk, Becker," Magriet had said. "You'd better get yourself to bed. You're going to feel like hell tomorrow."

"Tomorrow," Becker had said. "Tomorrow you can tell me what to do. Today I am a bachelor."

Magriet's father had watched her slam down the phone. "At least you have your education to fall back on," he'd said.

Magriet handed the photo back to Rose.

"You must find Beauty a nice black husband in America," Rose said.

Magriet hooked up her feeding bra and handed the baby to Rose. She got on the phone and finally located Becker at work. He agreed to come home for lunch so they could talk. Rose prepared a tray of sandwiches and tea. Magriet decided against taking it out to the garden, because she hadn't yet done anything about the pool, and the sloe-black water would not be conducive to conciliation. The dining room table was neutral. That would do. Rose would go outside with the baby, and Beauty was going to take charge of Kate. She undertook to help Kate dress up, complete with makeup, to be Princess Diana.

Kate's desire to be Princess Diana was Magriet's icebreaker when Becker came home. "She and Beauty have been watching the wedding tape all morning." She wanted to kick herself for reminding Becker of Beauty's existence, but his thoughts had gone in a different direction.

"You know what Kate said to me the other day?" he asked.

"What?" Magriet said. She bit into her sandwich and swallowed some tea.

"She said, 'If you knew the baby was going to make Mama so cross would you even have mated?'"

Magriet choked on the food in her mouth. She wanted to laugh at Kate's cleverness, but her humiliation at being criticized brought the hot sting of tears. She stirred her tea.

Becker sliced his sandwich into sickle-shaped slivers with his spoon. "I wanted to tell you this when she said it, but you were talking to Rose or something. You're never available."

"I'm not having an affair," Magriet said. "There are reasons for not having sex other than getting it somewhere else."

Becker looked up. "I can't think of any. Tell me." Then he went back over the sandwich and halved each piece.

"Small things can make a difference," Magriet said. She started telling Becker about the book she was reading. "There is this equation they use to simulate the long-term weather. If they change the parameters the slightest bit—but still use ordinary temperatures and pressures—a very different equilibrium is reached. What is so strange, is that this alternative climate has never existed in the entire geological past. Which is just as well, because in this equilibrium there would be no life on earth."

"That's why we're not having sex?" Becker said.

"They call it White Earth," Magriet said.

Rose burst into the room. The baby was on her back and she dragged Kate as royal bride by the hand. "It's Beauty, Ma'am."

"What's the matter, Rose?" Magriet asked.

"The policeman took she pass."

"A policeman?" Becker asked. "In my house? They can't do that. Not even in this country."

"No Master," Rose said. "Not here. Beauty she walked to the shops."

"Beauty is a princess too," Kate said.

Becker got up and went through the motions of tucking his shirt into his pants even though it hadn't come out. "Where is this policeman?" he asked.

"She don't listen to me. I told her there's trouble on the street. The policeman, he saw she pass is not right. He put it in his pocket. He said she must sleep with him, he'll give it back."

"What do you mean she pass—her pass is not right," Becker said.

"I'll deal with this," Magriet said. She was lifting the baby out of the pouch on Rose's back.

"I told you not to let her stay," Becker said.

Magriet thrust the baby into his arms. "Stay with Daddy," she said. She said the same thing to Kate. To Becker she said, "I'll be back soon. Please." To Rose she said, "Get Beauty. Get in the car."

Beauty came out of Rose's room with her head down. She was wearing Magriet's silver Matric mini dress. Liquid makeup had lightened her face to the color of white-bread toast. Crying had smeared her mascara.

They drove up and down the street, the policeman was nowhere to be seen. Rose got out and talked to some people, and after following leads for over an hour, Beauty spotted the man. Magriet double-parked and told Rose and Beauty to stay in the car. From a long way back an anger came that made her feel invincible. She walked up to the enterprising officer of the law. He was black and very young. He was an easy man to confront. She scolded him as if he were a child. She berated him for using his authority to exploit women. She told him to turn out his pockets. He did what she said. She was the white madam. Bypassers stopped to watch the spectacle. They cheered as she took back Beauty's pass, and the passes of half a dozen other women. "I am going to report you," she said, wagging a finger at him from inside the car. The onlookers laughed.

She did not report him. Back in the car she was shaky and nauseous. She gave the passes to Rose, who would put out the names at her church.

At home she shouted hello, but no one answered. Her legs felt wobbly as she followed the sound of the baby's screams to the backyard. Her breasts stung like a paper cut from the milk flowing in response to the wails.

Becker held the baby under one arm like a rugby ball. With his other hand he was wielding the pool net to get Kate's frog out of the plane tree. Kate saw Magriet first. She cried and ran toward her. "Daddy shouted," she said.

Becker handed Magriet the baby and Kate the toy. "Now don't throw him so high again, Kate," he said. He shouted to be heard above the baby. To Magriet he said, "Everything's under control." He knelt by Kate and talked in her ear. Magriet wanted to cry, but it wasn't the right time. The baby was deafening her with his toothless anger.

She walked away, holding him from her at arm's length. He flailed arms and legs, a baby astronaut. She was his lifeline. She made for a garden chair and unbuttoned her breast. At first he was too angry, but then he took it. He fell asleep immediately. When she went inside to put him in his crib, she met Rose in the doorway to Kate's room. Rose held out the Matric dance dress in front of her by its spaghetti straps as if it were a dirty diaper.

Magriet cupped her hands around her breasts. "The Punzi was too tired to drink, Rose. What am I going to do with all this milk?"

"It is Beauty who brought all this trouble to you, Ma'am," Rose said. "I must beat her."

Magriet felt a fissure opening up inside her. Her spiral into an inner vortex of absurdity was so desperate she was surprised at the sound coming from her mouth: she was laughing. The last she saw of Rose was when she turned from the door, still holding the dress, bewilderment weighing her down like a cross. Magriet made it to bed. She crawled under the covers and listened to the wet and salty gasps coming from herself. Gradually the sounds became dissociated, and she let herself float in the great white noise that superseded them.

After what seemed like no interval Becker's voice drew her out of the quiet. "You didn't hear the baby, so I fetched him. It's almost morning."

She pushed herself up on an elbow. "Good god," she said. "I did not say good night to Kate."

Becker put the baby next to her, and he started rooting for the nipple even before she got her blouse open. His snuffling triggered such a sting, she was as eager to nurse as he. "Did Rose give Kate her supper?"

"No," Becker said. "Rose was sulking, she wouldn't come out of her room. I made us some scrambled eggs."

"Didn't Kate ask for me?"

"She helped me clean the pool. You should hear the things she says. She was throwing that frog up in the air again, and she said this to me, exactly: 'Daddy, why is it so that if you throw something up it always comes down?' Can you believe it?"

Magriet smiled in the dark. "So I suppose you explained gravity."

"Yes," Becker said. "I told her about the moon. I threw her up in the air to show her how high she would be able to jump on the moon."

"Those footprints of the astronauts," Magriet said. "They're still there. They'll be there for millions and millions of years, just like we saw them that day."

"There is no weather on the moon," Becker said.

Magriet found Rose in the kitchen, later when it was light. She was scraping at some baked-on egg on a pan with her fingernail. When Magriet said her name, she dropped her hands under the sudsy surface of the water. She stared through the window. Her gaze was fixed on the far garden wall.

"I'm sorry, Rose," she said. "I wasn't laughing at you."

"You can laugh at me, Ma'am," Rose said. "I am the bad mother. Beauty she's the bad girl."

"No, Rose," Magriet said. She took a dishcloth and picked a cup from the draining board to dry. "What I did was bad. I'm sorry I laughed. I was tired."

The unforgiving blankness of an entire continent lingered behind Rose's eyes. Magriet swallowed. She wanted to tell Rose why she laughed, but she could not. She didn't quite know herself. It had something to do with the strange sensation she'd had at the moment when Rose threatened to beat Beauty, a sensation of having turned into her father: *You can put on a monkey a golden ring, / But it always will be a stupid thing.* She was immediately shocked at her thought; she'd imagined she'd risen above her father's views. But she had thought it. And she could not explain that to Rose. So she told her something else, although, she hoped, this would turn out not to have been the case. "Rose," she said, "there was a bad spirit in me last night. The master—Becker and I—have big problems. The master thinks I don't love him anymore."

Life returned to Rose's limp hands. She shook off the suds and reached for the other end of Magriet's dishtowel. From outside, concentric shivers of light from the surface of the pool enclosed the women in their parallel arcs. "I will pray for you, Ma'am."

JANUARY, 1985

Late one night, even though she had to be up early for Kate's school and her work the next morning, Magriet was downstairs working on her new computer. She was not using the accounting program. That she had not yet figured out. But she had found a word processing program and learned enough to use it, albeit somewhat gingerly. She was writing her life history. As she read what she had written, she wished she could think of less formal words. The Americans wouldn't like her stiff-sounding sentences. Feeling like a foreigner, she resumed her work.

She heard a sound, stopped typing, and listened. There was a hesitant knock on the door. She peered through the peephole before opening. It was Becker. She let him in. He looked around the living room as if he had forgotten the location of the furniture, and then sat down in an easy chair. Magriet took a seat on the couch.

Becker spoke. "Our green card went through."

A knot tightened around Magriet's heart. "When did you hear?"

"Last week."

She did not ask why he had not told her sooner. She took a cushion out from behind her back and cradled it on her lap like a baby. It was one her mother had made from goosedown harvested on their farm. By now most of the filling had escaped from a hole in the cover.

"It's up to you," Becker said, "what happens next. You can divorce me now."

Magriet folded the cushion in half and in half again like a pillowcase. She did not say anything.

"Or," Becker said, "you can come back from that angry place and forgive me."

JUNE 1981 THROUGH MARCH 1982

Rose did not beat Beauty that time. She informed Magriet she was going to spare the rod. "God will punish her," she said confidently. While waiting for the fulfillment of her expectation, she forbade Beauty to leave the room or speak to anyone. It was only when her pastor Terence came around that Beauty was allowed company again. Rose showed Terence into the room to take up Beauty's sins with God.

Terence, Rose told Magriet, was the answer to her prayers. He took his responsibility seriously. He ministered to Beauty every day, and every night Rose had some progress to report. One afternoon Beauty repented. The next day she gave her heart to the Lord. She was going to be baptized before returning to the teachers' college. Magriet drove mother and daughter to the shops to buy white poplin so Rose could sew the dress. Magriet and Becker and the children were invited to the baptism, and they went, and took pictures of Beauty beaming in her white dress like a bride, the latter being a comparison both inappropriate and curiously apt, as became apparent during Beauty's next vacation four months later when, upon being scolded for having become too fat for the poplin dress, she confessed to being pregnant. It was then that Rose beat her, until Beauty named Terence, the pastor, as the father. But what Magriet remembered even more vividly than Beauty's screams from the servant's room, was Rose's almost inaudible admission of defeat in the kitchen the next morning: "Now she will never be a teacher like you, Ma'am."

When Beauty's time came she gave birth to twins. There had been no question of her marrying Terence, because he already had a wife and five children. So it was Magriet who fetched Beauty and the babies—with their unpronounceable Tswana names—home from the hospital, home to Rose's room, where they were going to hide them. Rose did not go along in the car. Someone had to stay home to look after Kate and the Punzi.

Rose was waiting when Magriet pulled up in the driveway. She unlocked the gate, but did not come out. Beauty was in the backseat holding the babies. Magriet, who had been coached by Beauty on the way home, swung open the back car door and announced, "Thamavunda and Thamavundyana."

Rose looked at the paving stones instead of into the car. "Terence oughten to have given Beauty twins," she said.

Magriet took the nearest baby, the tea-with-cream one, and Beauty got out of the back seat carrying the other little girl. When they got to the gate, Rose could no longer keep her eyes averted. She looked. She darted forward. She dumped the Punzi at Magriet's feet and gathered up Beauty's babies, one in each arm. She named them Pretty and Patience.

JANUARY 1984 THROUGH DECEMBER 1985

Although Magriet could now find a legal job, she continued with her babysitting and cleaning. She told herself the little boy in her charge had become used to her, and she could not abandon him now.

She often thought of Rose. News reports of disruption in her ex-country increasingly appeared in magazines. Almost daily the violence was shown live on TV. She wanted to get in a car, a plane, and find Rose. Find Beauty. And the babies. Which was impossible. They had lost contact. On the morning of the day they had left for America, there had been a pass raid at the house with the pool. Beauty had been taken. The babies, who were in the house when the men came through the gate, had been over-looked.

As reports of violence in South Africa escalated, Magriet experienced an increasingly urgent need to talk to Rose. One day, casting frugality to the wind, she phoned a former neighbor to inquire about Rose. The rented house had been sold and demolished, a movie theatre was going up in its place. The neighbor had no idea what had happened to the old girl.

Magriet thought if she could have afforded the plane fare, she would have gone over there and looked for her. But she had no money. Her work money was a pittance, and something kept her from looking for a better job. In an odd way, staying in her current job brought her closer to Rose than if she would have actually spoken to her. She felt in many ways she had become Rose. Becker had been right, she thought. She and the children were poor whites now. Somehow she found the thought comforting.

Becker, too, seemed strangely content. She had never given him an answer about the divorce, and he had not asked again. He spent a lot of time with Magriet and the children. One day, after Magriet had so thoroughly scoured and swabbed her employer's house that the smell of disinfectant remained embedded in her body even after a shower, they sat on the couch together after the children had gone to bed and started touching and kissing. They made love. But when Becker asked if he could move back home, a whiff of Clorox from her skin evoked the chemicals that she never did put in the pool, and the murky algal water surged and engulfed her, washed her up breathless against the Johannesburg house's kitchen window as if she were pressed against the pane by a large hand from behind.

MAY, 1982

It was the week before Magriet and her family were to leave for America. Rose and Beauty were helping to pack last-minute things. The babies were on Rose's and Beauty's backs as usual. Even when not tied to someone's back the babies spent most of their time in the house, because, Rose had insisted, pass officers are not allowed to come into a white house. Magriet took Pretty (she was the dark one, her skin the color of cinnamon bark, like Rose's) from her mother and sent Beauty to fetch another box. As Magriet cradled the baby, endearments rolled from her mouth in familiar cadences. She did not arrest the occasional "Mama's baby" that spilled out with the piggies and the punzis. When the baby's eyelids opened and closed like the wings of twin moths and her infant body went limp with sleep, Magriet kissed her on the head and laid her down on top of some sheets in a packing crate. When she looked up she noticed Rose had been watching her. A familiar expression of gloom, the one Becker referred to as Rose's sulking face, set the crinkles around the older woman's mouth into uncompromising lines. "You must take her with you to America," Rose said.

Magriet picked up a lumpy object wrapped in newspaper and started undoing the wrapping. Her throat felt tight, as if she'd accidentally swallowed one of those candies they used to call niggerballs as children and was waiting for the painful peristaltic contractions to finish forcing it down. She rewrapped the object without having noticed what it was. She placed it on the bed, walked over to the dresser to fetch her and Becker's passports from the drawer. She showed them to Rose. "She does not have a passport for America, Rose," she said.

"Babies don't have passes," Rose said. "The Punzi and Mizkatie—where their passes?"

Magriet explained. "They're written in on mine—on their mother's."

"Then you write Pretty in there too."

Magriet did not reply. She was thinking how to explain without hurting feelings that Pretty would not pass for her and Becker's child when Rose burst out laughing. "Pretty, she's too black. You gonna have to take Patience."

Ashamed that she always underrated Rose's poker-faced intelligence, Magriet joined in the laughter. She took up the joke. "In America it does not matter what color you are. She can go to school with the Punzi."

Rose took over the fantasy. Patience would get a good education, she said, become a teacher. And then she would send for her sister and her grandma.

That was when Beauty spoke up from the door where she

had apparently been watching. She almost seemed like the old Beauty, after having been quiet and withdrawn ever since coming home with the babies. "They teach us by the Teacher's Training," she said, "that you cannot separate twins."

On the night of their bon voyage party at the Greek restaurant, this story got Magriet the attention of all her friends.

"We must seem above the law to them," Marianna said.

"We *are* the law," Becker's friend Barry said. "We're white."

"Especially you, Magriet," Rick said. "Wrestling down a cop for those passes." (That story too had been revisited, and Magriet's role had been jokingly enhanced.)

Laughter enclosed the party in an envelope of congeniality.

Barry shook his head. "The things they latch on to," he said.

It was only Becker who was grim-faced. Later, in the privacy created by the shatter of plates hurled into the fireplace, he said, "You've let this thing with the servants go too far. You're giving them expectations."

Even though Magriet turned from Becker without answering—it was her turn to smash one of the cheap plates the restaurant provided for merrymaking purposes—his words stayed with her that night, a nagging mantra behind her shallow sleep. The next day she had more people to say good-bye to, and was distracted, and it was only on the morning of their departure to America when she again had occasion to consider Becker's accusation.

She went into her son's room to dress him for the airplane. He was not the only baby in the crib. On either side of the bulky one-year-old lay tiny Pretty and Patience. Or what appeared to be Pretty and Patience except for the ghastly beige of their faces. Instead of the chocolate cake and cinnamon toast tones by which the babies were easily distinguished, masks of makeup reduced them to indistinguishable caricatures. They were dressed in their Sunday bonnets and aprons, and from each of four frilly sleeves a petite makeup-lightened hand flailed toward the solar system mobile overhead. If Magriet had been in any doubt about the meaning of the tableau before her, her uncertainty was dispelled when she noticed leaning against the crib legs an outsize diaper bag with "Pretty" and "Patience" embroidered across the top.

Becker had been right.

Magriet's heart clamped. How could she face Rose? *I did not mean it Rose. It was a joke.* How could she tell her? *It is against the law.* Disordered and disparate formulas swirled chaotically in her head.

It took Magriet's rational mind an instant to fix on her only possible recourse. The babies had to go. Beauty had to go. Becker was right. This thing had gone on too long. She never should have let them stay.

She was calm. Her hands did not shake when she picked up the phone book and turned to the Government Pages. Her fingers did not falter when she underlined the Pass Office number. Her arm was steady when she picked up the receiver. It would be better this way. They would only be locked up a night or two. Then they would be sent to the country, where it was, after all, healthier for children. Soon they would be too big to be kept indoors all the time. There they could play outside, run in the sunshine. They would be fine. She would give Rose the money to pay their fine. She and Becker were, after all, also victims of the system.

After dialing the sequence of numbers, after giving the address to the voice that answered, she finished dressing her son. Her thoughts were very systematic. She would leave him in his crib, and walk outside with the babies, stand with them in the backyard, ask Becker to take a picture. She would just happen to be there when they came. Rose would never guess. Her movements became faster, more deliberate. People said they came quicker than cops to a crime scene.

Just how true that was, she discovered as she was carrying the dirty diaper to the outside garbage can. By the time she got to the back door, before she'd reached her arm around the corner to lift the lid, she was halted by the screech of tires at the gate. Her thought that the padlock would forestall them lasted only a second. The gate had been left unlocked, Becker had been in and out putting stuff in the car all morning. Men in khaki uniforms rushed into the yard, and pushed open the servant room's door. Their shouts were underscored by a soprano scream from Rose.

Magriet dropped the diaper and stood immobile in the door. As the noise level rose to a crescendo, disbelief at what she'd done weakened her legs so she had to support herself against the door jamb. Thankfulness that she was not holding the babies was the only truth about herself she would not doubt later on. Now that a familiar-seeming drama was developing before her eyes, a drama that had played in her imagination only minutes before, fear that the travel-ready babies in Rian's crib would be discovered was her overwhelming emotion.

One white and two black officers were standing guard at the servant room's door. Others were inside, and the bark of their voices mingled with the high wail of women's protest. With the ease of a dream image the white officer broke away and was transported to Magriet. He had reason to believe, he said, an illegal was being harbored on the property. From inside Rose's room came shouts in which Magriet could distinguish only the word *pass*.

At that moment Becker came up behind Magriet where she was rooted in the kitchen doorway. "What the fuck?" he asked. When Magriet turned around, her heart cramped with dread. He had Rian on his hip and a twin cradled in the crook of his other arm. Kate squeezed between them, the other twin clamped to her chest with both hands.

The white officer took a step closer. He cast his gaze on the family, smiling.

Kate took a step forward, perilously eased herself into a sitting position on the step, and held out the baby. "Patience is Princess Diana," she said.

The officer put his hands on his hips, bent his head toward Kate. "Pretty sister you have."

"No," Kate said, "Pretty is with my dad."

Becker looked from Kate to Magriet and back at the little girl he was holding.

The officer laughed. "You're all pretty," he said. Then he turned to his men, who were leaving already, pulling Beauty with sleep-wild hair, Beauty in shorty pajamas, between them. Her eyes were wide with terror, but she did not make a sound. Rose followed behind, trying to drape a dressing gown over her daughter's shoulders. Her mouth spilled garbled prayers.

Magriet put her arms through Kate's from behind and lifted both her and the baby into the kitchen. She shifted the baby up onto Kate's shoulder, adjusted her daughter's hand to support the baby's neck, and then she went outside again.

"Where did Beauty go?" Kate asked.

Becker turned from the door and went inside. "Stay with Daddy," he said.

After the van had driven off, after Magriet had prised Rose's hands from the gate, she led her into the kitchen. She pulled out a chair at the table and eased Rose onto it. Rose was silent now, a tear path shining darkly on her cheek.

Kate was whining. "Where did Beauty go?" she repeated.

"That girl," Rose said. "She walked to the station last night. Someone see her. She don't listen to me."

Magriet pressed down on Rose's shoulders, not so much to comfort her as to stop her own hands from shaking. Her eyes were on Becker. "You left the gate open."

Becker sucked his bottom lip into his mouth to show he was not going to say something he would later regret.

"Patience is too heavy," Kate said.

Magriet stepped in and eased the baby out of Kate's grip.

The view from Rose's chair would have been this: the family lined up in the kitchen on their last day in Africa. The master, his face stern as a patriarch's, but his demeanor belied by the armful of children; the madam, the good mother, suspending a baby in midair at arm's length; the girl, hands like steps beneath the feet of the baby in transfer, her gaze already fixed on her father who is speaking. From this distance the damage already done to the babies' whiteface by drool and tears did not show. Frozen in time this episode remains a repository of hope. It is nothing more than a family gathered together, about to have lunch, maybe, the nanny about to take the punzies from the master and play with them in the back so the parents can have their food in peace.

Time, however, does not stand still. This scene, after all, is a tableau vivant. So the child in Magriet's hands traversed the distance to her chest, and rooted there for something to suckle. Kate ran out of the room to fetch her frog. Becker put both of his babies down on the floor, and spoke:

"I'm not paying the fucking fine."

Rian crawled over to Rose and pulled himself to standing on the pillars of her legs. Rose did not see him. Her gaze went over his head and out the window where, like all of those from whose eyes the scales have dropped, she must have perceived dark bursting like sunspots into the golden glow of the day. Her voice, when she spoke, channeled hopelessness from the continent beneath her feet. "The trouble of Beauty is not your trouble, Master. It is mine." She got up, picked up the babies, and carried them to her room. Then she came back inside and carried Magriet's and Becker's suitcases to the car.

Magriet met her at the gate as she came back. Magriet had

taken some of their travel money from her overnight bag—in front of Becker—and stuffed it into Rose's apron pocket. "Write to me Rose," she had urged.

Rose's eyes were cast down, fixed on a spot between her feet. "No money for stamps," she said. Those were her parting words.

And if that is where Rose's story essentially ends for Magriet, her own goes on and that is what she must live with.

FALL, 1986

When Magriet's employer decided to return to school and moved away, Magriet gave up her domestic job and went back to school herself. She needed only a few classes to certify as a teacher. Soon she was once again teaching math, this time at a high school named for the sixteenth president of the United States, Lincoln, a fact she knew because she had acquired a citizenship booklet, and was mining it at night, while sitting at the kitchen table after grading her papers, for guidance on loyalty and trust, their roots, and who was allowed to feel love, and toward what and whom.

Some weeks after she had started her teaching, she slipped away during lunch to attend *Where in the World Day* at Rian's school (he was a kindergartner now at John Adams Elementary), and was observing her son join his class in pledging allegiance to the flag of the United States. She did not participate. Unlike Rian she knew she had to pass another test before she could put her hand on her heart. She felt between her breasts for the throb of response, for a drumming patriotic affirmation, but found there merely a faint pulse, a questioning flicker that asked how a new allegiance to a whole new country was possible when certain old ones among just a few people had been impossible to sustain.

Suddenly she did not know if she wanted to become an American. She shifted her weight in the desk usually occupied by a child Rian's size. She wanted rather to be like Einstein, who, after renouncing his German citizenship, declared himself a Citizen of the World. She knew she was no Einstein (even though, like him, she'd taught herself Euclidian geometry at the age of twelve). The world would not clamor to receive her. If she wanted to belong anywhere, she realized, *she* would have to make the promise to love and abide.

Becker appeared in the classroom door. Rian was up in front of the class already, unfolding the zebra skin Magriet had, without Becker's help, untacked from the wall, because Becker was still only a visitor in his family's house. He looked about the room for a place to sit, and although there were parent-sized seats open near the front, he made a makeshift chair of a wooden craft table to be close to her.

They sat side by side listening to Rian tell about South Africa. He held up the zebra skin. "Zebras are a kind of striped horse. No one knows if they have black stripes on white skin, or white stripes on black skin. They used to live everywhere, but now they live in the Kalahari Desert. The pioneers had guns and they shot them. My dad did not shoot this one, we bought it." Everyone clapped, and then it was the next child's turn. A pretty girl wearing wooden shoes and leading a grandmother-aged woman in a rose-print dress by the hand was clomping to the front.

Becker was looking at Magriet. He leaned toward her and whispered behind his hand: "Magriet? It's time."

Magriet put her finger to her mouth and pointed to the front of the classroom.

Becker took a folder from the seat behind him, took out a page with a child's drawing, and wrote on the back. He passed her the note. *Picture this,* it said. *You're standing in a desert. The Kalahari. No clouds. Everything is featureless. It is light, but the sun cannot be seen. Everything is totally symmetrical. For you to begin a journey, a step taken in any direction would be as good as one taken in any other. But as soon as you take a first step, you leave a mark in the sand, and this means one direction has been singled out from all the others.*

She felt his eyes on her face as she read it, and somewhere below her breastbone emotions sprouted like ferns in a time-lapse documentary. She brought a hand to her mouth, and from behind it, said sweetly, "You were *destined* to fuck that woman."

"No," Becker said, forgetting to lower his voice. Heads turned, Becker coughed. He started to speak in a loud whisper, and to make themselves less conspicuous, she moved her ear up to his mouth. "This is science," he said. "I'm explaining the arrow of time. Rian called me this morning while you were making breakfast. This is what he asked: 'Why is it if you put the egg in the batter and stir, and then stir backwards, the egg does not get back together again?' Can you believe it?"

"He phoned you in the middle of breakfast?"

"He phones me every morning," Becker said, "before school. Yesterday it was hyenas."

In front of the class the girl, a paper fan in each hand, held out her arms to the sides so the patient grandma could tie on her sash.

Magriet screened her mouth with her cupped hand. "He wanted to know if they could smile."

Becker nodded. He leaned in closer. "It was urgent. When you got to know, you got to know twice." His breath was a hot wind in the labyrinth of her ear.

Magriet looked away toward the flag curled next to the window. They left a Stars and Stripes on the moon, she remembered. In the absence of air it required an aluminum frame to keep it unfurled. It would be there, like that, until someone went back to get it. Except—

We do not live in a stable universe. A comet could knock it over. Even the solar wind. Turbulence lurks everywhere, and the bat of a ricepaper fan in the hand of a girl dancing to the thin reed of her grandma's song could set off a storm of cosmic proportions, could send a farmhouse in Kansas spinning to the sky. Or it could churn up forgiveness in a human heart, send it caroming around the room like a five-year-old on roller skates.

In the children's circle, Rian swiveled back in his chair and waved. Magriet turned to Becker. "You should have seen the two of them this morning," she murmured. "When Rian asked about the eggs, Kate explained the arrow of time with Humpty Dumpty."

Becker took his note from her and drew doodles around his writing before whispering back: "All the King's horses and all the King's men / Could not put Humpty together again?"

She aligned her mouth with his ear. "I thought that was too grim, so I added my own examples of irreversible transformations. A tadpole turns into a frog. A caterpillar becomes a butterfly." She drew back, watched his face.

He stared at her, a questioning look spreading like a smile from his mouth to his eyes. "The frog turns into a prince?"

Her thoughts rushed out the window, skeetered along the clouds, came to a halt half a world away. "Some people think we shouldn't teach fairy tales anymore," she said.

He didn't move, but there was no peace in his stillness. Hurt, rather, in the way he slouched. Under his half-day growth of beard, a muscle shivered.

She leaned closer, her arm touched his from shoulder to wrist. His cheek was a cratered landscape too close for focus. "But I," she said, "I disagree."

She felt more than heard his lips brush her name against her cheek. "My Griet?"

She took his hand and lifted it to her heart.

Walking Legs

The BMW's backseat is crammed with ranunculi and chinkerinchees and chrysanthemums. I balance a bunch of gardenias between my knees. They poke through the steering wheel. They bob to the jazzy blast from the radio. Some township band. At the turn into our driveway, the sheaf of strelitzias topples over from the passenger seat and slaps me in the face. I coast to a stop just inside the gate. No point in driving into the garage. There are the flowers to deal with first. Heady with the essence of blooming things and wet newspaper, I loosen my tie and sit for a moment savoring the engine's drone beneath the diminishing pulse of the music. The announcer's hype cuts through the dampening sound. The news will be next, he says. Be sure to stay tuned for the latest on Mandela's release. A date has been set.

I turn the key to off. After stuffing a short-stemmed bunch or two into each of my blazer pockets, I get out. Then, leaning back in, I gather up the rest of my offering. It is not until I straighten my back and turn around to elbow the back door shut that I notice: I am face-to-face with a goat. Or rather, its head. Some-one has stuck a goat's head on the corner post of the fence divid-ing our place from Tshabalala's.

I don't usually get to see death this fresh. I'm a paleontolo-gist. Usually I get my animal fragments valorized by time. This one looks as if it isn't even cold yet. Even so, I take note. Careful *in situ* observation of a specimen enables one to infer certain parameters of the habitat. One ear points up and one sideways in an asymmetry that is mimicked by the drift of the eyes. There is no tongue. A dried meander of blood leads from the mouth to the neck edge, where a still liquid drop quivers. The surface dulls as it crusts over. A fly crawls from a nostril and buzzes my flow-ers. I am reminded of the task in hand.

At the front door I adjust my load and fumble for my keys. I am trying to be quiet. I want to make it all the way to the bedroom, put flowers everywhere, and then shout for Christine. I want her to be surprised, to gasp when she walks in. My arms must be free to hold her when she sees what I have brought.

Inside, my attempt at stealth is stymied when I tiptoe past Christine's heirloom clock. It registers my passage with a sustained metallic twang. Christine detects the sound, even though the TV is on. "In here, Eckles," she shouts. She is in the living room. She has been my girlfriend for a year. We live in her house.

I backtrack and stop in the door frame. One of the double doors is closed. Burdened as I am, I don't fit through. Through a gap in the foliage I see Christine on the floor by the coffee table, with her back against the couch. Our neighbor Tshabalala is seated on an easy chair across from her. As always I start when I see him there. The way I've been brought up, if there's a black person and a white person in a room and there's a chair and someone is sitting in it, it should be the white person. But this I try to get over. I'm an educated man.

The backgammon set Christine has given me for my birthday is set up between her and Tshabalala.

"Guess what," Christine says. She waves toward Tshabalala, who has been her regular backgammon partner since he moved in next door after the referendum last year gave him the right. Black neighbors were a new thing in this upper crust suburb of Johannesburg, but everyone was determined to rise to the occasion. Christine immediately invited them over to tea, setting a special table with her childhood tea set for the four little girls we'd seen peeking through the fence. But no wife and children came. Only Tshabalala. He did not want tea. His eyes strayed to the bottle of White Horse on top of the liquor cabinet, and after several polite refusals he was persuaded to have a shot. He paced the room taking small sips and clinking the ice against the side of the glass. He picked up a die from the backgammon board where Christine and I had been playing, and asked what game it was. We told him, and taught him the moves. The next day, when he came back for another game, we found out that he seems to have heard *black*gammon. That's what he asks Christine to play almost every day. They are playing again now.

"Hello Doc," I say. Tshabalala owns a medical supply

company that has the monopoly on Baragwanath, a government hospital described on his business card as "the biggest medical institution for blacks in the free world." Doctor Tshabalala was on TV for having chartered a plane to bring over a team of nurses from Taiwan to train at "his" hospital. He himself paid the salaries of four white doctors to head the goodwill project.

"Eckhard, my friend," Tshabalala says. He is a large man, fiftyish; he has about ten years on me. *Soft parts can only be preserved by a stroke of good luck. Insects in amber. Sloth dung in a desiccated cave.* Tshabalala hefts himself from the chair and comes to my aid. He opens the other half of the door, and lets me in. He catches my eye through the flowers. "We have a proverb," he says, laughing. "Beware of white men bearing gifts."

"African wisdom," Christine says. But she gets up from the floor and kisses me past the cat's claw that the flower seller has thrown in for free. In an ear-whisper that gives me gooseflesh she says, "Flowers aren't what I want."

We go into the kitchen. I put the flowers on the counter and start looking for hollow things. Although I have lived here for a year, I still don't know my way about the cupboards. In Christine's house the staff are in charge of towels and sheets, vases and bowls. The only reason I get as far as opening the pantry door myself, get to breathe the closed-up air as I scan the shelves, is that the kitchen maid Sarah has taken a dislike to Tshabalala, has made it an in-your-face gesture to take to her room whenever he darkens our door. When asked to account for her rudeness, Sarah said, "He is uncouth." But Christine, who had more information than I to go on, saw right through her. She accused Sarah, a Zulu, of not wanting to fraternize with the Tshabalalas because they were Tswanas. From the sullen closing off of Sarah's face, she told me later, she knew she'd hit the problem on the nose. She followed this insight by lecturing Sarah on the necessity for all South Africans, even Zulus, to learn to get along with their neighbors. Sarah replied with a freedom of speech that predated the election, that derived from her status as Christine's nanny. "What do you know of Tswanas?" she said. "You white." Christine, indignantly outraged, reminded her that she had joined the ANC even before the election, when whites could still be jailed for belonging. Sarah was not impressed. "Those Mandela people no different from the government," she said. "They just different teeth in the same mouth."

Christine, who could not bear to be permanently at odds with anyone, went over this conversation with me time and again, trying to dredge meaning out of Sarah's metaphor. Whatever else I got out of this hermeneutic exercise, I realized that my continuing relationship with Christine entailed being on friendly terms with all her friends, including Tshabalala. That's not hard. I usually don't mind him, or his house calls. I just wish he'd make them when I'm not here. With him around, and Uncle Broer who lives with us, sometimes it's hard to get a word in with Christine.

It looks, now, like we're going to have a moment alone. She follows me into the closet-sized storage space. As she reaches for something over my head, I breathe the intimate aroma of her underarm. I butt my head into the curve her triceps makes with her breast, but she nudges me away.

"Doctor has invited us to a party," she says. She speaks too loud for the space, indicating with meaningful thrusts of her head toward the kitchen that Tshabalala is within earshot. She has a cloisonné jar by the neck with one hand, and dangles a Delft jug by the handle with the middle finger of her other hand. "Andrew is coming home."

It has been about two months since we first heard about the existence of Tshabalala's son Andrew. We were in bed, Christine still on top of me, with the radio on an oldies station as usual while we were making love so Uncle Broer would not hear. The song—a Neil Diamond medley, I recall—was interrupted by a news flash. Winnie Mandela's bodyguards, known as "the Mandela United Football Club," had kicked a thirteen-year-old boy named Stompie to death, while she allegedly looked on. Another young man was also assaulted, but he survived. A miracle, the announcer said, since his esophagus had been severed with garden shears in a failed attempt to slit his throat. Although he had also received severe leg injuries, he had managed to pull himself by his arms along a fence for about a hundred yards, after which he was found and taken to the hospital. The man's name made us pull apart and sit up. It was Andrew Tshabalala.

Christine immediately phoned next door. Doctor Tshabalala was not home, and the woman who answered barely spoke English. Christine got no answers. The next afternoon Tshabalala came over as usual for his game. The injured man was his son, he said, the one with the Master's in political science, the one just back from Oxford. He was at Baragwanath, getting the best care money could buy. Tshabalala would not discuss the extent of his injuries, or his prognosis. He met every question with, "He going to be fine." Christine decided to show our support, to at least send flowers, but when she started phoning around there was no one who would deliver to the townships. It's too dangerous, they said.

Now in the pantry Christine's voice is raised to a determinedly upbeat pitch. "A welcome home party for Andrew," she explains. I try to read her face, but in the half-light the nuances of her expression are erased.

"That's nice," I say.

Christine bites her lip and looks the other way to where light from the kitchen slices into the dimness of the pantry. She squeezes past me and steps back into the kitchen.

Tshabalala is there when I exit. "We don't have anything tall enough for the strelitzias," I say.

"A celebration," Tshabalala says. "The return of my first-born."

"Tomorrow, all day," Christine says. She fits a bunch each of the yellows and reds into the containers she'd found. The rest she masses in a mixing bowl. "Maybe all weekend. Get Doctor a drink. We're going to finish our game."

"Wilcox and the American are coming over tomorrow," I say. Christine shrugs her shoulders and walks back into the living room. I run water into the sink for everything that's left.

"They can come too," Tshabalala says from the door. "The more souls, the more joy."

I look back to catch Christine's eye, but she is gone. She is only in the next room, but she already feels far away. Yesterday she got a letter with a job offer from an American she met last year at the Zurich airport during a layover. A job in America. What every white South African wants. I think she will go. She wants me to go too.

"What about—this," I asked last night when she told me. I made a gesture that she took to indicate the gazebo we were in, the floodlit pool, the house.

"I'll sell it," she said. "While I still can. Mandela is going to take it anyway."

I did not answer. I had intended my gesture to be more encompassing. To extend even beyond Christine's estate, beyond her latest project, the neighbors. To include the faraway hum of traffic on Jan Smuts Avenue. The chatter of the bush-babies in the trees overhead. The Southern Cross, whose long arm points toward a rocky outcrop at the outskirts of the city with an eight-foot-thick lens of shale at its heart that draws me like a lodestone. But to Christine *this* refers to the things she owns, the real estate she wants to transform into moveable assets. I don't blame her for that. Bad things have happened, have crusted over her possessions like flowstone. What I blame her for is thinking, though she's never said it, that if she rids herself of her things, leaves her possessions behind like the rich young man in the Bible is urged to do, it constitutes some kind of injunction for me to follow her, to see it as an occasion to prove that I love her for herself. Whatever people might think, I'm not with Christine for what she has. Not the material things, anyway.

"What about Uncle Broer?" I said then, last night in the gazebo. Uncle Broer is Christine's father's brother who lives with us. It would probably be more accurate to say that Christine and I live with Uncle Broer. Christine inherited him along with the house and her parents' *HIS* and *HERS* BMWs. Or rather, the house and everything else will be Christine's when Uncle Broer is no longer with us. Uncle Broer has the usufruct. In practice that does not make too much difference. Christine is the one in charge, because money is just one of the things Uncle Broer does not have a sense of. But Uncle Broer is more to Christine than a responsibility. The debt she owes him is a moral one.

When burglars taped Christine's parents into their hammocks a year ago and poured petrol over them and set them alight, Uncle Broer was the one who filled the ice bucket from the pool time and again and who, with meticulous fairness of alteration, tried to douse the parallel fires. Uncle Broer was not able to tell why the intruders left him to his task, but it is easy to imagine them laughing and shaking their heads as they loaded suits and jewelry and appliances into their truck: no one perceives Uncle Broer as a threat. "What about Uncle Broer?" I said again.

Christine was staring toward the side of the pool where she has had to have the grout between the paving stones replaced because the soot embedded in the grooves from when the hammocks crashed down from their moorings would not wash out. "Uncle Broer is not the problem," she said. "Uncle Broer will go where I go."

I felt accused. Uncle Broer was hardly a standard. Uncle Broer would go with anybody. Moreover, Uncle Broer was able to carry the possessions he valued on his person like a Bushman. So could I. Possessions aren't why I wanted to stay. Time was. I needed a year, two maybe. To excavate my site, put my name on my discovery.

It happened just before I met Christine. At the time I thought I had completed my work at the quarry. I did not need any more fossils. After two years I thought I had a representative collection of that particular death assemblage. Interesting insofar as anything is interesting that lived that long ago, but nothing unexpected. Yet, one day after work I went back there for another look. It had become a habit. I was absentmindedly tapping at the face with my hammer when a piece of shale the size of a footprint loosened into my hand. I eased it out of the bed. It opened like a book onto an imprinted shape that caused me to suck deep of the cool air. At first I thought it was a fluke, an effect of the last daylight slanting over the ridge, like the face on Mars. But when I turned the rock surface to where the sun had just set, it was unmistakable: the circular symmetry: the three equal, radiating, hooked and tentacle-fringed arms: *Tribrachidium.* Only one other specimen was known, from the Ediacara site in Australia. It was an entirely anomalous creature. Nothing like it had ever been seen among the known millions of animal species.

I wrapped the two halves in my handkerchief and carried them back to my car. I went straight to the museum. Found the Ediacara slides. Drilled off a sample of black to send with Max to Wits for carbon dating first thing in the morning. Started thinking about finding money to quarry some more. One fossil doth not a species make. Six months, maybe, to see if there are more. Three, with luck. Another year or two to reconstruct. Three years to publish.

That was a year ago. I still haven't raised the money. But I was closing in on it. The American would be here the weekend. So last night when Christine told me about her job, I had a hard time acting happy. "Why now?" I asked.

Christine got up out of her chair and walked to one of the gazebo's arched openings. She supported herself with a hand on each side pillar, like someone who had no strength left. She had her back to me. "You know what was the worst about what happened?" she asked. "It was what people said to me. 'What can you expect—they are savages,' they said. 'How can we let people like that take over the country?' they said. 'We should have killed them all off like the Americans did with their Indians.' And it did not even occur to me until the Tshabalalas moved in—no one knew for sure if the people who did it were black or not. Uncle Broer did not say. No one asked him. But we all assumed it. And we are probably right. But that's not the point. The point is that here you do not even ask."

What could I say? I did not agree with Christine about how bad things were here. The people who killed her parents were ordinary scum. Criminals. Thieves. They weren't making a political statement. There are people like that in every country of the world. But how can you argue with someone who has kept the suitcases her parents were packing for their next trip—to the Greek islands—open and undisturbed on their bed for a year? I could not think of anything to say. I walked up behind her and looked over her head up at the sky. "In America you won't have the Southern Cross." I slid my hands down and up along her upper arms, then down again so my palms were pedestals for her elbows.

The night sky is, as it were, one of Christine's things. She'd told me about the Southern Cross before: it was only named as a new constellation in the seventeenth century. Ptolemy doesn't mention it in the *Almagest*. But he does name Orion. Orion is an old, respectable member of the zodiac. It can be seen from all five continents. Christine must have been thinking of the same conversation. "I'll have Orion," she said.

Astronomy must be the only science more irrelevant than paleontology. But don't say that to Christine. She is a volunteer fund-raiser for the planetarium. This is not just an honorary position. Christine works hard at, as she calls it, spreading the light of knowledge. She does slide shows at business clubs, signs up sponsors to give township kids free field trips to the star shows. She baits the fat cats with her erudition, she says. Last night she dangled a morsel of fact before me, too. "Orion: in the northern hemisphere he'll be right side up."

"I like him on his head," I said. I took her by the shoulders and turned her to face me. "Sometimes arse over heels is good. First the honeymoon, then the wedding."

Christine's sudden start told me she knew what I was referring to. On the bulletin board in her office upstairs she has left undisturbed her mother's twenty-five-year-old newspaper clipping with a picture of John Lennon and his fiancée in white pajamas. *Beatle Star Hitched—Yoked by Ono*, the caption says. The article tells of the "love-in" that preceded their wedding.

I'm old-fashioned at heart. I would have married Christine within a week of meeting her. She was the one who had asked me to stay, not for herself, then, but because Uncle Broer would not let go of my hand. It did not take long before she, too, would not let me go. There was the funeral. The reading of the will. The estate, the taxes. Relatives scuttling out of their mining company houses with their claims. Her ex-husband. The endowment trust, the charities. By the time it was over, it had become clear to her how good I was with sorting information. Getting the big picture. That's my job. To me, at the same time, it had become clear just how much money there was between us.

I'm old-fashioned, as I've said. There was no way I could provide for her in a manner she was accustomed to. I had a good job at the museum, but I was no Tshabalala. Nevertheless, I had made up my mind to ask. By now Christine and I have been on honeymoon, so to speak, for almost a year. It was time for a wedding.

I'd been fantasizing about asking her. The where and the how. The gazebo, I'd thought. A spray of jasmine from the trelliswork for her hair. A ring in my pocket: amber. Last night I had no ring, but that was not the reason I did not ask. I did not want to make her think I'd only come up with the marriage idea to dissuade her from going to America. But I was thinking of marriage. And then my thoughts took off on one of those stupid trains of associations that led from one useless idea to another. And where it ended was that marriage was a prerequisite for widowhood. John Lennon had a widow. The thought surprised me. I said it out loud. "Yoko Ono is a widow."

Christine looked at me the same way Sarah had looked at Tshabalala when he'd put out his cigarette in the shell of the African Aphrodite sculpture. She would not talk to me after that. She pulled away and walked toward the house, slowly at first, but with an increasing pace, so that by the time she reached the patio she was running. Away from me. The door slammed, a muffled thwack that suspended the night song of the frogs and crickets.

I got into my car (Christine's father's car, to be exact. The *HIS* BMW. She had given it to me so it would not just sit in the garage. Uncle Broer does not drive). I let down the hand brake, let the slant of the driveway take me silently down to the street. I started up the engine and drove out to my rocky outcrop in the south. I needed time, large chunks of it, to get back in touch with the big picture. I quarried by flashlight. Even if I found something, I would not know till later. The stuff I work with is nothing spectacular like you'd see in a rock shop. Just black messes on rocks. A paradox of soft-bodied creatures is that although the soft parts are wonderfully preserved, the body contents seep out into the surrounding mud. So it takes me over a year to scrape the insides from the outsides in order to reconstruct even one species. To restore a number of black stains to the semblance of something that once was alive, alive as a species for millions of years before it became extinct. Dinosaurs were around for only a third as long as my creatures: a mere 100 million years. Humans don't even get figured into the time scales I work with. *If the age of the earth from its origins to the present time is imagined as equivalent to a single day, then man appeared less than a minute from midnight at day's end.* In my profession's scheme of reckoning man is negligible. Woman is not even mentioned. *Homo sapiens* is a trivial part of the thin film of mammalian life smeared over the surface of the planet since the Paleocene. *O Earth, what changes hast thou seen. / There where the long street roars, hath been / The stillness of the central sea.* And so on: my thoughts shaped themselves like clouds, dissolved like Tennyson's solid lands.

Not until day spilled light over the horizon did I call it a night. When I stopped at a traffic light on my way home, I was accosted by a flower seller. I bought every flower in her stand.

Now in the kitchen the dawn tints of the strelitzias against the draining board jolt me back to the present. The strelitzias are getting squashed by their own weight. I stand them up against the window. Delicate structures vein their stained-glass colors. Nothing of what I see would ordinarily be preserved in a fossil. But every aeon or so there is a miracle. A soft-bodied fauna is kept from decomposition. Not just one organism, but hundreds. Thousands, maybe. Each one mineralized cell by cell. Discovered and excavated about five hundred million years later. By someone like me. A bright kid from the wrong side of the mine dumps who nevertheless got an education because he was white. But that was in the old South Africa. Now that they're letting Mandela out, things are going to be fair. The money that used to go to science is now going to electricity for Soweto, to free medical care for pregnant women. Paleontology has become another bourgeois intellectual pursuit. That is why I will have to resort to Wilcox. He is honorary curator of the Goldfields Museum. Wilcox has connections. Wilcox has a plan. He has dreamed up an educational TV series, he says, that will do for the Paleozoic what Steven Spielberg has done for the Jurassic. An American from Theodore, Alabama, is putting up the money.

I pour two glasses of wine and a whiskey, and carry them into the living room.

"Thanks, Tully," Christine murmurs. She lifts her glass to me. My name is Eckhard, and usually she calls me Eckles. Tully is a good sign. It is the name associated with a recent intimate moment, a name she picked up from a picture in a monograph I was reading in bed some weeks ago. She shifted her head onto my pillow, and read, "*Tullimonstrum.*" She twirled a pinch of my chest hairs into a dreadlock. "What's that?"

"A bizarre wormlike animal," I said. "Latin doggerel for the Tully Monster. It's extinct."

She moved her hand from my sternum to my crotch in an exploratory manner. "No, it isn't," she said. With her other hand she switched on the radio. Afterwards, while we were still breathing hard, the news about Winnie Mandela came on.

Now at the coffee table Christine passes the doubling cube to Tshabalala. "Double."

I cringe. Sometimes Christine can be so reckless. They play for money. Tshabalala pays in rand, but lets Christine give him coins that she lets him pick from the bucket where her parents had for years emptied their pockets after returning home from exotic destinations.

Christine has a man on the bar and Tshabalala is bearing off when Uncle Broer comes in with a bug for me. But it is Tshabalala who gets first dibs on Uncle Broer.

"My brother," Tshabalala says. He works through the complicated triple-grip handshake of black power with Uncle Broer. In slow motion. That's how one does things with Uncle Broer. "How's the knee?"

Uncle Broer hitches up his pants leg with his free hand and displays a fits-any-curve band-aid that Tshabalala imports from Germany. "Not off yet, Doc-torr," he says. He looks pointedly at Tshabalala, and then at me, and says, "Doc-terr." I have explained the difference between a PhD and an MD to Uncle Broer. It is easy in Afrikaans. One ends on an -or and the other on an -er. What is harder to explain is that Tshabalala is neither. His father named him "Doctor" with prophetic trust, but he turned out to be a businessman. This I told Uncle Broer, but Tshabalala's band-aid proved more convincing. "Doc-terr," he repeats to himself until his eyes fall on the bug between his fingers. He holds it up to my face so close it is out of focus. "Doc-torr," he says. This time his pronunciation indicates he means me.

Uncle Broer knows that my work consists of piecing together squashed bugs that I find between slabs of shale. At first he brought me rocks, pointing out insect-shaped features. But then it must have struck him that whole bugs might save me a lot of time. "Thanks, Uncle Broer," I say. I down my wine and pop the insect into the glass. It sticks to the side. I turn the glass over onto the coffee table. Uncle Broer and Tshabalala and I examine the scrabbling beetle.

"Ab-do-men," Uncle Broer says. He jabs at the glass with a forefinger.

"It's missing a right proximal walking leg," I say.

"Doesn't miss it much," Tshabalala says. "Got plenty more."

"Six," Uncle Broer says. Then he lists the body parts to which the leg pairs attach. "Pro-thorax. Meso-thorax. Meta-thorax." Droplets of his spit spritz onto the upturned glass. He beams a wet grin in my direction.

"*Walking leg* is a taxonomic term," I say. "*Leg* is an anatomical, not a functional term. Not all arthropods use their legs for walking. Insect mouth parts, for example, are slightly modified legs." I get a laugh out of Tshabalala. I look at Christine for approval. I'm making an effort here. But she's not smiling. She looks pensive. Uncle Broer not only smiles, he laughs out loud. His pleasure does not derive from the idiosyncrasies of language use. He gets high from the words alone. "Tax-o-no-mic," he says, holding the word between teeth and tongue before letting it go. "Me-so-tho-rax." He finds more words on the inside of the backgammon box. He reads them out loud. Christine sips her wine.

Tshabalala rattles the dice. He throws a double six and bears off the last of his men. "Gammon," he says. He picks four coins from her parents' stash. "Come to the doctor," he says.

The American's name is Ray Keller. We are dangling our legs in Tshabalala's pool. Wilcox is sitting nearby on a kitchen chair because of his suit. Ashes from the barbecue fire settle like a design on his navy alumnus tie. He blows at them. Knowing Wilcox's fussiness I guess he is dying to flick them off, but he needs both hands for the safekeeping of the American's video camera, with which he has been entrusted. Keller now jumps out of the pool because something filmworthy is happening. The woman Christine and I have dubbed "the second Mrs. Tshabalala" shouts in Tswana as she turns the roasting goat. Several other female helpers and Uncle Broer are assisting. "Pakamisa," they shout. "Pezulu." Keller rushes over to capture the moment. Like Christine, he is making memories of Africa.

I swim to the middle of the pool, where Christine and Tshabalala are on blow-up chairs, with a cork backgammon board bobbing between them. "How many of those do you have now, Doc?" I ask. He has built up an amazing collection in the six months since he learned the game.

"Too many," Tshabalala says. He lunges for the doubling cube, which is floating away on my waves. "I was naughty. But I couldn't resist. Only five hundred dollars in the duty-free at Kai-shek."

"That Wilcox is an idiot," Christine says. She points to my boss, who is following the American to the barbecue pit while dragging along his chair.

After listening to Wilcox courting Keller all morning, I happen to agree. Wilcox is not interested in research. He wants to magnify and colorize and animate my fossil creatures until they sell better than Tyrannosaurus Rex. He wants to put a posable arthropod next to every dinosaur on the toy store shelves. However, now is not the time to own up to Christine. I turn to Tshabalala. "How would you like to come in on a deal with us Doc? Educational programs. A TV on every street corner in Soweto."

"The new South Africa," Christine says. "With freedom, dignity, and TV for all. I'm tempted to stay."

"Stay," Tshabalala says. He may have missed the irony of her tone, but I haven't. "Mandela will soon be free."

"Did you see the cover of *Time?*" Christine asks. "The face of a man who hasn't been seen for twenty-seven years."

"It's very scientific," Tshabalala says. "They made him older with a computer. Like those missing children on TV."

"They made him look like Nancy Reagan," I say. "His head's too big. Like a puppy's."

"How would you know?" Christine says. "No one has seen him, except Winnie. And she says it looks like him."

When it comes to inferring a morphology from bone structure, I am on solid ground. That is what I do. I have seen a picture of the young Mandela, although looking upon his likeness had been forbidden since the fifties. His photo was banned, available only via the underground. When I discovered the tea boy at the museum had one taped to the inside of the broom closet—this was in the days before the referendum, when it was still illegal—I should have reported him. But I didn't. I was curious. The youth of the man in the photo was what had surprised me—he was almost seventy in real life, by then. When rumors were being circulated in the tearoom that he would be released, I extrapolated that skull through twenty-seven years. At first I did it in my head, but lately I have made some sketches.

Now in the pool I am not given the opportunity to display my erudition. Tshabalala is exploding in a fit of dark rage. He spits past the backgammon board. "Don't say that woman's name in my presence," he says. "Fuckin whore." He slides off the floating chair and strikes out for the side.

"Winnie," Christine says. "The mother of the nation. With a special interest in the physical education of our youth."

"Nothing has been proven," I say.

Christine kicks over the board. "I don't have your belief in proof," she says. "I go by my gut."

"Look at the big picture," I say. "Winnie's got guts. The ones with guts are the ones who survive."

She slides off her chair and locks her knees around my waist under the water. "Come with me to Michigan. It's a beginning. A new beginning. And Stephen Jay Gould lives there."

"So does Mickey Mouse," I say. "Uncle Broer will like it."

"Mickey Mouse doesn't live in Michigan," she says.

"The Magic Kingdom," I say.

"What do you have against Mickey Mouse?"

"Let me tell you about Mickey Mouse. His head's too big. And the way he cleaned up his act is suspect. He used to be a bad guy. In his first cartoon he was a bloody sadist, in fact. He made music by torturing animals. He pulled a goat's tail to make it sing. He used a cow's teeth for a xylophone. He tweaked a pig's nipples and played bagpipes with a cow's udder. And now they've made his head bigger, so he looks innocent. Like a little kid."

"So that's so bad?" she asks. "What does that prove?"

"He's been sanitized. That's what happens in America."

"Sanitation," she says. "This whole fucking place can do with some sanitation. And you've got just the man for it." She gestures in Keller's direction. He is videotaping Wilcox in conversation with a strikingly beautiful woman in the kind of African dress you see only in boutiques. "He's going to do a Disney on your project."

"I am Africa's biggest expert on the Paleozoic," I say. "I have the final say."

"Paleoterrific," Christine says. She flops backward and leaves me to gather the dice and men bobbing with haphazard energy in her wake.

I decide then and there I won't go to America. Ever. It has nothing to do with my work. Fossils will wait. The way things are going, no one else is going to quarry my *Lagerstatt*. Or any others, for that matter. Which may be just as well. For the next while, fossils may be safer in the rock than out. Unless someone who is capable of seeing the big picture takes charge around here, almost a century of work is going to go to the dogs. Is going to be prettied and twisted and served up as entertainment by Wilcox and his ilk. I'm the only one who can stop it. Once I could have left the country, independently of Christine. I have had my own job offer. It was from an American university. "We are extremely impressed with your monograph," it said. "We don't often see reanimation of this quality." They know the way to a man's heart. Reanimation. Imbuing the dead with life. You can't just look at a dark blob on a piece of shale and render it as a complex, working organism by mindless copying. It takes genius. You start with a squashed and horribly distorted mess and finish with a composite figure of a plausible living organism. It takes spatial genius. I have it. I can move from two to three dimensions and back again. But not to America. This country needs people like me.

Uncle Broer is how I met Christine. I got to know him long before I knew she existed. I became acquainted with him at the Goldfields Museum, where I had just been appointed Keeper of the Catalog. On my first day, on my way in, I noticed a man lurking behind the mastodon in the foyer. He followed me to my office, keeping a guilty distance, and peeped around the door a few times while I arranged my things. He was wearing a suit. His tie had Mickey Mouse as astronaut on it. When Max the tea boy came, he explained about Master Broer. I was to give him records to copy. That was what my predecessor Dr. Dyson used to do. While Max went back to the corridor to coax Uncle Broer inside, I got Wilcox on the phone.

"There is a Mr. Brewer here," I said. "Max tells me he is part of my job description."

Wilcox laughed. "Mr. Lawson, actually. Of the AfriGold Lawsons. Broer, as in Afrikaans for brother, is his first name. We all call him Uncle Broer. When Dyson left, he explained to him that he was retiring, and suggested Uncle Broer do the same. I guess the advice didn't take. Just give him something to do. AfriGold is one of our top donors."

The name of the museum's benefactor company rang in my ears like a siren. AfriGold sponsored the boardinghouse for mine orphans where I was sent after my father was killed in the Western Deep accident of '62.

Max led Uncle Broer in by the elbow, and introduced us. His suit pockets were bulging with rectangular shapes whose outlines pressed through the fabric. Recording tapes, maybe. Or a month's supply of cigarettes. We shook hands.

"My work please, Doc-terr," Uncle Broer commanded with impeccable manners.

I looked around, unprepared for this unexpected new duty. I killed time, explaining that I was actually a doc-torr, until my eye fell on a shelf of notebooks labeled "Klippan Exc." I picked the one marked 1951, because that is the year I was born. I handed it to Uncle Broer. He opened it at random and studied the page.

"O-ny-cho-pho-rans," he read. He handed the book back to me. "Finish," he said. He distractedly patted his suit, then extracted three identical notebooks, each the size of a pack of cards, from an inside pocket. He leafed through one, licking his forefinger at each turn. Page after page of impeccable italic script passed in and out of view. After an interminable interval he thrust the notebook up to my face. "There," he said. His finger marked a copy of the word he had earlier read.

I sat him down across the desk from me. Three shelves down we found him a volume he had not yet copied. He excused himself, looked nervously at his watch, and left the room. At four thirty he returned the field notes, with the wrapper from a chocolate bar marking his place. He put the volume sideways on the shelf for easy retrieval the next day.

From that day on Uncle Broer was a daily visitor to my office. Sometimes he would pick up the notes, remark on having fallen behind, and immediately disappear to wherever he did his copying. On other days he would visit, sharing his chocolate bar, and his handkerchief for wiping our hands afterwards. On these occasions we had long conversations about our work. I explained to Uncle Broer what I did, and from what he showed me I gradually gathered that he mined the field notes for nice-looking words. When he found one he liked, he measured it against the cap of his fountain pen. If it was as long or longer, he copied it over.

At first, I will admit, it was indebtedness to the Lawsons that kept me civil toward Uncle Broer, not so much for what they did for me when my father died, because that was the least a company should do for the child of an employer sacrificed to its profit margins, but for the salary the museum could not afford to pay me other than through AfriGold's sponsorship. After some weeks, however, I began to feel a bond other than obligation apropos Uncle Broer. He sort of felt like family. Family was something I'd never really had, except in the ontogenetic sense. Later, when Christine would ask about my family, I would tell her this joke:

A traveler stopped at a farmhouse to ask the way. A boy of about six opened the door.

"Where's your dad?" the stranger asked.

"At work."

"Out in the fields?"

"No. There are no fields," the boy replied. "It hasn't rained for seven years. My dad is working on the mines."

"Your mother?"

The boy explained that his mother had taken to drink during the drought, had fallen into the pit toilet one day and drowned. His grandmother then looked after him until grief made her mad, and she was taken to the asylum. A childless aunt next extended mercy, but when she had her own baby she sent the boy home where he now was the landlord of a family of black squatters whose food he shared.

"Any brothers or sisters?" the stranger asked.

"One brother," the boy said.

"And where is he?"

"At Wits."

"The university? You have a brother studying at Wits?"

"He's not studying," the boy said. "He's in a bottle. He's got two heads."

Christine would not find this funny. But that was essentially the story of my life. I was that boy. Or maybe I was the brother with the two heads. At any rate, I ended up at Wits. And then at the Museum, where I found myself looking forward to my daily sessions with the man that would turn out to be Christine's uncle.

One day, when Uncle Broer did not return the notes by midafternoon as usual, I was edgy and could not get on with my work. I was about to make inquiries when he suddenly stumbled in. He had the posture of someone wearing a straitjacket: his arms were crossed over his chest and his hands thrust into his armpits. He mouthed incoherent words and sentence fragments. When I failed to understand him, he reached out a hand and pulled me by the sleeve. His hand was blackened, and raw with burns. I followed him the six city blocks between the museum and his house—a house that, by the time we got there, already technically belonged to Christine under the terms of her parents' Last Will and Testament.

Keller shouts my name from the direction of my house. His head appears over the fence, next to the goat's. He beckons for me to come over. A trail of children follow me into my yard.

The first Mrs. Tshabalala is sitting in one of my flower beds. She pulls up a plant and adds it to the heap on her lap.

"What is she doing?" Keller says. "Ask her what she's doing."

I have lived in South Africa all my life, but I am just as incapable of communicating with Mrs. Tshabalala as Keller is. We have no language in common. But I have picked up the local lore about the natives' ability to live off the land. Keller will like it. I pull up a weed. Beet red veins and bottle green leaf. *Smarag* is the Afrikaans for a green of this color. "To us it's weeds," I say. "To them it's food."

Keller waves me into position next to Mrs. Tshabalala. He wants to film our conversation. "Talk to her," he directs.

"Thank you for weeding our garden," I say. I grope for the snatches of Tswana I picked up as a child. All I remember is how to count. "Utuku, kobedi, orari." It seems to make Mrs. Tshabalala nervous. She arches her back in preparation to leave. "No, no," I say. I gesture for her to stay. I give her my weed. I smile and pull up more weeds, but it is the camera I talk to.

"Johannesburg is situated on the Witwatersrand, or Ridge of White Waters, the basin where the gold is found. Somewhere beneath my feet is the Carbon Leader, a layer nowhere thicker than the width of my hand. That is where the gold is. Under the microscope the carbon is seen to be formed of millions of lichen-like plants that caught the heavy gold particles as they dropped out of the flowing water. Nature panned out the gold in a way men would invent two billion years later when they discovered how to wash crushed rock over corduroy in a stream of water." I add the weeds I have collected to those already in Mrs. Tshabalala's lap.

"Morog," she says.

The word rings a bell. "African spinach," I say.

Some of the younger Tshabalala children elbow themselves into the picture. They hold *morog* plants out like flowers and fix their smiles. Their eyes follow Keller's waving hand.

"Tell them to sing me a song," he says.

They don't wait for me to translate. This is the new generation. They understand. They stand up straight and sing *Nkosi Sikelele l'Afrika, God Bless Africa*. This is a song that was banned for as long as I remember, and now some black kids are belting it out on my front lawn. This is a new era. Things have changed. I want to shout for Christine, make her listen, but the voices start faltering. The singers are fixated on a pickup truck, laden with people, that is driving by slowly. When the truck stops at their house, the song breaks off. They rush toward the newcomers. "Andrew," they shout. "Andrew is here."

"Andrew," Mrs. Tshabalala says. She holds a hand over her

mouth, and I can see it trembling. With her other hand she folds her topmost skirt up over the bundle of *morog*. When she is done, she reaches out to me and I pull her to her feet. Supporting the bulge on her stomach as if it were a pregnant belly, she shuffles to her house.

Keller and I follow, but first he pauses for a close-up of the goat's head. It is starting to stink. But it should look great on film. The aubergine of dried blood and the green iridescence of blowflies. Exotic Africa.

When I get back to the party, Christine grabs me. She holds me tight. "I love you," she says.

"What's the matter?" I say.

"Come with me to America," she says.

"Hey," I say. "We'll talk. Let's meet the miracle son."

She pulls away from me. "I've met him," she says. She runs across the lawn and into our yard.

Relatives make way for me around Andrew Tshabalala. He is sitting on a straight-backed chair next to his father. Uncle Broer is standing behind him like a bodyguard, holding a briefcase. The young Tshabalala is in his late twenties, closer to Christine's age than mine. His face is a darker black than his father's.

"Eckhard Odendal. Pleased to meet you," I say.

"This is Andrew," Doctor Tshabalala says.

Andrew nods his head. His handshake is firm. He turns around and takes the briefcase from Uncle Broer. He takes out a notebook and writes something. He hands it to his father, who reads, "Proletarian efforts of many pig police. Right on."

I laugh. What Andrew has written down is a memory device made up by one of Stephen Jay Gould's students, for remembering the epochs of the Tertiary period. "Paleocene, Eocene, Oligocene, Miocene, Pliocene," I say. I mentioned it on TV recently when I was on a science panel after I discovered my *Lagerstatt*, when I had my epoch of fame. Andrew could have seen me. Even so I wonder why he is telling me this. I have heard about doctors—the medical kind—who get accosted at parties by people who tell them their symptoms or show their suppurations in order to extract a free diagnosis. But, as everyone including Uncle Broer knows, I'm not that kind of doctor. The stuff I know is not even remotely useful to anybody, except for making conversation.

So you're a paleontologist?

Yes. That's like an anthropologist, only you're looking for a different number of feet.

So that is how I take Andrew's communication: one educated man making small talk with another. There's nothing the matter with small talk. That's what Christine always tells me. That's how we're going to learn to communicate in this country.

"I have a better one now," I say. "It reviews a porno movie. Listen to this. '*Cheap Meat* performs passably, / Quenching the celibate's jejune thirst.'"

Andrew's hand on my arm stops me. He hands his pad to me, and jabs it with the pencil to show what he wants. I write down the entire mnemonic. It works from recent to early, chronicling all of the great dyings of life on earth. Uncle Broer leans over me and reads each word as it appears from under my pencil. When I get to the epilogue for the epochs of the Cenozoic, he is unable to keep still from pleasure. *Rare pornography, purchased masochistically. / O Erogeny, Paleobscene.*

Andrew laughs with hissing and panting sounds. The older Tshabalala watches him. Tears run down his face. One of the bystanders puts a hand on his shoulder and leads him away. Andrew's forehead beads with sweat. He drains his glass, and empties the ice down his shirt. He writes on the pad. Uncle Broer reads. "What. Do. You. Call. A. Person. With. No. Legs. Hanging. On. A. Wall."

Tshabalala senior returns. He has a bottle in one hand, and is taking long swigs from it. He pauses to fill up my glass. "I will kill him," he says. "I'm going to find him. Then I'm going to find her. And kill her."

Andrew waves his pad for attention.

I say I don't know.

Andrew writes.

Uncle Broer takes the pad. "Art," he reads.

Andrew hisses. He writes some more, and draws an arrow up to his earlier joke.

"Same," Uncle Broer reads. "Question. But. Also. No. Head."

I shrug my shoulders. "Beats me," I say.

Andrew snorts and chokes. He pulls down his turtleneck and shows me a bulging scar across his throat. It looks as if an annelid has been grafted onto his neck. He writes the answer.

"African. Art," Uncle Broer reads.

Andrew mimes laughter with wide open mouth and scrunched-up eyes. He tears the top page off the pad, crushes it, and drops it on the ground.

Uncle Broer rescues the crumpled page. "*Cheap. Meat*," he reads. "Erogeny."

Andrew jerks his head up in surprise as if he is noticing Uncle Broer for the first time. He turns back to look at him over his shoulder, then swivels back and works his mouth as if trying to speak out of long habit. The mirth is gone from his eyes when he gives up and grabs for his pad. "What the fuck," he writes on a clean sheet, "does this kind of doggerel have to do with Africa?"

I happen to agree. "You're absolutely right," I say. I start telling him about a movement among South African earth scientists to develop a terminology more germane to our part of the world. I have had not a small part in defining nomenclature appropriate to the southern land masses, that, after all, had been remote from the northern hemisphere events for which the eras and epochs have been named. "I think it is wrong," I said, "that Kazakhstan and Bohemia are represented in the geological record, and not South Africa. So this is what I did." I gesture that I want the pad, and he hands it to me.

It takes me a long time. I do a sketch of the arthropod that has made me famous—as paleontological fame goes. It is my favorite creature. I have named it for the new South Africa. After Azania, the name the blacks have decided we'll be known by. *Chimerazania*. No one knows which end of it is up. Or down. Or front. Or back. For my monograph I reconstructed it from several actual specimens. I was bent over the camera lucida and microscope for over a year. It was like reanimating a cartoon character flattened by a steamroller. I am good at making sense of disjointed bits and pieces. Except I still don't know which side is the head. Perhaps *Chimerazania* had no frontal mouth at all. Perhaps each tentacle gathered food independently through its own mouth and passed the collected particles down its own personal gullet into the communal gut.

At first Andrew looks puzzled. Or maybe he's just thinking his own thoughts. When I'm done, he seems to have cheered up. He writes *Good work!* next to my sketch. He draws a smiley face. He draws a star.

Tshabalala brings us each a chunk of barbecued goat. Fat runs down Andrew's chin. Fat drips on *Chimerazania.* When Andrew has eaten his portion down to the bone, he tosses the remains to the ground and takes up the pencil. "The man who cut me—his name is Xoliswe Falati," he writes. This time it is Doctor Tshabalala who reads every word as it comes out. "They say he fled to Botswana. But I'm sure he didn't. Geoffrey saw him at the funeral on Monday. The Mandela bitch was also there." He taps his neck with the pencil.

"Xoliswe Falati," Uncle Broer says. "Paleobscene."

Christine is back. She stands across from me with an armful of flowers. "I hope you don't mind," she says. "But I would like to give these to Andrew."

I shrug my shoulders. "Fine with me," I say. "Whatever."

Christine turns to Andrew. "Welcome home, Andrew."

Andrew smiles and writes gracious things on his pad. Uncle Broer reads them. I take the flowers from Christine and lower them into the pool onto the shallow step. I work the string off a bunch of ranunculi and toss each flower separately into the center of the pool. I realize I have always wanted to do this. *There are three preconditions for the preservation of soft-bodied organisms: rapid burial in undisturbed sediment; deposition in an environment free from the usual agents of destruction; and minimal disruption by the ravages of heat, pressure, fracturing, and erosion.* I see that Keller is filming me.

"Old African custom," I shout.

When it is dark, the glow from the pool's red underwater light attracts those who are left like a campfire. Doctor Tshabalala has passed out and has been carried inside. Uncle Broer is asleep in the middle of the lawn on two blow-up chairs pushed together. Christine has gone home to watch an anniversary special on the Beatles.

Andrew and I are by the poolside passing a bottle to and fro. We are not conversing, because the light is too bad. From the kitchen the women's voices blur into sounds of cleaning up. After a while the first Mrs. Tshabalala comes out and walks slowly toward Andrew. She hands him a parcel wrapped in newspaper. He opens it and holds it toward the pool to see. He laughs, or maybe gags, and hands it to me. It is a body part of human proportions, so it takes me a second to realize its origin is probably the goat. It is a tongue.

Andrew covers it back up and puts it in his pocket. He writes on his pad and hands it to me. I dip down to the water surface to catch more light. "I need a doctor," I read.

"I can take you," I say. I wake Uncle Broer. He washes his face and hands with water splashed up from the shallow end of the pool, and when he is done he takes the other side of Andrew's chair. We carry him to our driveway and load him into my car. Uncle Broer gets in the back. I am in the driver's seat. "Where to?" I ask. I switch on the overhead light so I can see Andrew's directions. Soon we're on the way to a place I've never seen, a place not shown on any map of the Witwatersrand, although it is Johannesburg's conjoined twin, a city of a million people that goes by the acronym for South Western Townships. When the streetlights become sparser and the road surface increasingly bumpy, Andrew leans over and switches off the inside light. This way, I imagine, I am a less likely target for the legendary barrage of missiles supposed to greet whites who cross over the great divide. In the backseat Uncle Broer has resumed his nap.

From the craters and pockmarks that suck shadows from the headlight beam I infer the roadside scenery: trees and shrubs fall away, and rows and rows of subeconomic housing units tessellate the landscape like the postapocalyptic shelters of a low-budget space movie. We pass the turn-off to Baragwanath. The idea I have harbored that the hospital is where I am taking Andrew, is extinguished. When the highway narrows into a suburban road, more of the surroundings become visible in the yellow glow of anticrime floodlights. We have entered the black suburbs.

Close-up the houses that appear identical in the police heli-
copter view from which my mental picture derives are differen-
tiable by a fence, a rose bush, a purple front door. Andrew reads
these signs, and nudges me around turns and in and out of back-
tracks. There are no street names. I soon abandon my attempt to
memorize the route in preparation for a sudden retreat, a possibility that lurks beyond my immediate perceptions—*I climb on the
roof and shout it out, my mother is happy when I kill a white*—like the
clusters of young men in the dark spaces between the lampposts.

When we enter a side street, a group of pedestrians block the
way. I slam on the brakes and wait petrified. Music other than the
engine's idling hum penetrates my awareness. The people visible
in the beam of the headlights are dancing. Andrew motions for
me to keep moving. He rolls down his window and sticks out his
head. He reaches out a hand and drums on the roof. I rev the
engine and inch forward. The dancers make way at the last possible moment, banging on the roof as the car passes among them.
Once we are through the crowd, we pass a car decorated with
ribbons parked in front of the house. I am embarrassed for having
been afraid. Even here beer cans tied onto the back bumper of a
beribboned car can surely not be indicative of anything other
than a wedding celebration in progress.

After a slow cruise to a house two doors farther along, Andrew
gives a thumbs-up signal and I stop. I wake Uncle Broer. I forgot
to bring the chair, so we position ourselves on either side of
Andrew, and he hangs on with an arm locked around each of our
shoulders. I knock, and a large man opens the door. "My brother,"

he says, and scoops Andrew from between us. He carries him inside, leaving me and Uncle Broer redundant on the doorstep. Inside several men sit around a table in a cone of light from a low-hanging shade. One of them motions for us to come in.

There is no sign of Andrew inside, but the man who carried him in appears from behind a bead curtain that divides the front room from one beyond. The bead strings incorporate mirror sequins, and their undulating reflections pulse across the walls and ceiling. In the far corner foam rubber mattresses are piled, with blankets and clothing on top. A liquor advertising poster with a bronzely tanned beauty on a white beach is the only wall decoration. I recognize the ambience. We are in a *shebeen*, the township equivalent of a pub.

The man who invited us in is named Halftime. With a heartiness I suspect is fueled by liquor he identifies himself as the regional secretary of AZAPO, which registers vaguely in my mind as something political. He indicates two vacant chairs and introduces us to several of the seated men. Rolihlala, or "Rolly to you whites," is the man who opened the door. "The Tutu man," Halftime elaborates, in what strikes me as a mocking tone. A collective groan rumbles around the table. I catch individual remarks along the lines of "Let it rest, Halftime," and "Put a tit in it." The protests fade into a low murmur when a woman in tight jeans and a shiny pink shirt appears balancing a tray laden with beer bottles. Individual attentions turn to counting coins into her outstretched hand. While I'm still fumbling for cash, she sets two beers down in front of me and Uncle Broer, and waves off my attempts to pay. Uncle Broer sits down and I am about to when the room is set aswirl with moving points of light. All eyes turn to the bead curtain where a woman has appeared, dressed in a leather apron and wearing a stole consisting of animal skins with the heads attached. From the lore dished up on the cultural TV programs since the election, I recognize her as a *sangoma*, or traditional healer. According to this source, no respectable black entertainer or businessman would dream of making major life decisions without consulting his *sangoma*. Since the election there have even been rumors about black trade unions demanding that time off work approved by *sangomas* should be subject to the same benefits as sick leave sanctioned by the medical establishment.

The woman comes up to me and holds out Andrew's pad. "The doctor does not read," Andrew has written. "Send in Comrade Broer."

I explain to Uncle Broer that he is wanted, and lead him to the curtain. The *sangoma* holds the beads to one side. Andrew sits cross-legged on the floor by a small fire. A crumpled sheet of newspaper on top is unfolding itself in the heat. As I watch, it bursts into flame, affording me a glimpse of the goat's tongue by Andrew's feet. Then Uncle Broer passes in front of me and blocks my view. The *sangoma* gestures that I am not allowed to follow. "*Cheap Meat*," I hear Uncle Broer saying.

I go back to the table and sit down next to Halftime. He is younger than he seemed outside the circle of bright light: early twenties, I guess. He leans over and holds out a calculator. "You got a spare battery on you?" he asks.

"Sorry," I say.

"Fuck," he says.

"What are you trying to calculate?"

"How long the Tutu man still going to live." He points to Rolly.

Rolly rises to his feet. "Fuck off, Halftime," he shouts. He punctuates his outburst with meaningful jabs of his beer bottle.

The man next to Rolly pulls him down by his shirt. He speaks across the table in a conciliatory tone. "Why don't you leave it alone, Halftime," he says. "It's Christmas since you lend the man your stuff, and you never missed it, so what's with you now?"

Halftime pushes his chair away from the table. "First he steal my suit. But now he fucking around with the imperialists. They stealing our struggle."

A murmur passes along the table. Rolly raises his voice. "You drunk, Halftime. You making politics out of everything. When you like this you can make politics out of Elvis."

There is general laughter around the table. There are shouts of "Elvis lives," and "Long live the King."

Halftime stands up and in the same movement swings his bottle out and down and knocks it against the edge of the table. There is a cracking sound, and when his hand appears over the edge of the tabletop again, it is holding a weapon. He reaches to the center of the table with drunken precision, and lays it in the center. "Everything is politics," he says. "There is politics in beer." He sits down and focuses on me.

"First they steal our sign," he says with a meaningful look toward the other side of the table. He clenches his fist in the black power salute and raises it overhead. "Now they stealing our songs." As his arm drops back down on the table with an impetus that rattles the bottles, he intones a tune. "*My mother is happy when I kill a white . . .*" His eyes lock in on mine for a moment, and the melody segues into a cackle. "You in politics, white man?"

"No," I say. "I work at the museum. I—I reconstruct animals that lived a long time ago. Like dinosaurs, but just smaller."

Next to me it seems Halftime has gotten whatever was eating him out of his system. Or maybe he is going to pass out. Elbow on the table he is supporting his chin in the classical position of the thinker.

It is Rolly who picks up the conversation. "Ah," he says. "Tyrannosaurus rex."

"Yes," I say, "my animals have just as much personality."

A man across the table smiles in my direction. "Personality doesn't count. Do your animals have teeth?"

Halftime rouses himself for a moment. "There is politics in Elvis," he says. "Elvis cannot be King. I already have my King. Biko is my King." He speaks softly, as if to himself. I think I am the only one who can hear him.

"My animals have teeth," I say. I tell about *Anomalocaris* with its crushing circular mouth lined with three concentric rows of teeth. There are grimaces and exclamations from the audience. "Auk," an old man on my left says.

"Jaws," Halftime says. This time his voice rises above the bluster of noise. "Now there is politics."

Everyone laughs. I don't get it. But I am exhilarated that something I can talk about has defused the situation. Christine is right. Knowledge is what we need to light up the darkness of mistrust. I bask in the privilege of this moment. I feel as though I am in the right place at the right time. Communication is the answer. The undivided turf of natural history is the place to get together. Rolly encourages me from the other end of the table. "What other animals you got?"

I tell about *Capetownia*, a creature that had a body the consistency of raw liver, and in whose gut I nevertheless found fragments of shells indicating that it had been able to crush hard-bodied prey. I tell about *Egolia* with its five eyes. By now I wish I had a pencil and paper, so I could show them. But I imagine the only writing materials in this place are in the other room. So I decide to keep talking. Let the words give the picture. "Then there is *Chimerazania*," I say.

Halftime wakes from his apparent slumber. "Azania," he says. "Your animal is called Azania. Now that is my kind of politics." He jabs a saluting fist at his adversary across the table. "He said Azania, Zim-zim man. You hear that? Azania."

Rolly thrusts himself from his chair and points his beer bottle at my end of the table. At first I think he's aiming at Halftime, but then Halftime gets up and stands protectively over me. So I get it that I am the one being addressed: "What you want with that BC shit, man. They won't even take you. You white. That shit went out with Biko. He just a memory, man."

I scramble my brain trying to reconstruct the events leading up to me being accused of something, but it is difficult to concentrate since Halftime is leaning over me and groping for his broken bottle. A charged silence has come over the room. Into this quiet a meteor of light bursts as Uncle Broer parts the curtain. "Pig police," he says.

Rolly twirls around as if he is being attacked. He swings his arm and the bottle in his hand catches the light. There is a splintery tinkling sound. Uncle Broer falls to his knees and clutches his head. Rolly's neighbor grabs him and they crash down on the floor in a flail of arms and legs. Halftime dives onto the table and slides across and over. "Run, white man, run," he shouts. Then he goes down head first on top of the fighting men. Others join the free-for-all.

Uncle Broer's high, desolate cry rises above the din. "Doc-torr. Doc-terr. Doc-torr. Doc-terr." I skirt the scrummage on the floor and go toward Uncle Broer. Two other men get to him before I do. I swing back an arm and aim for the nearest one's face. He catches me by the wrist and puts a grip on me that halts me dead. "Slow down, brother," he says. "I'm your friend. You got to get the old man out of here."

I don't say anything. I take Uncle Broer by the elbow. He gets to his feet. Slowly, the way he does things. One of the men walks on the other side of him. I scan the dark outside the trapezium of light slanting from the open door. A movement catches my eye. I glance about me for a weapon, but then I see it is Andrew. He is dragging himself along by his arms. The *sangoma*, now on his left, now on his right, seems to be propelling him forward with a torrent of words.

I put Uncle Broer in the back. The men help Andrew into the front. When I get in, he is slumped forward, his head resting on crossed arms. I wave at the men and shout my thanks. At the wedding house the bridal couple are just leaving. Their car is helped forward by people running alongside and slapping the sides and roof. My car is given a similar impetus. I focus on the fluttering ribbons and follow. Andrew is not giving any directions. His shoulders are heaving. In the backseat Uncle Broer whines and wails, and keeps asking for a band-aid. I soothe and make promises. "Things will be better soon," I say. "Things will be better when we get home."

I find my handkerchief in my pants pocket and hand it to Uncle Broer. His whimpers die down. The only one still crying is Andrew, but he does it quietly, with watery breathing sounds.

When I reach an area with larger houses and more streetlights, the bridal car pulls into a driveway, and the couple gets out. The woman is in a floor-length wedding dress and the man is wearing a tuxedo. I drive up behind them. I hate to interfere, but I have no choice. "You look very lovely," I say. "Can you tell me the way to the highway?"

"You are in Westcliff," the woman says.

"Orlando West," the man says. "Go back to that street over there. By the high school."

Andrew is stirring on the seat beside me.

"Daliwonga High School," the woman says. "Turn right. You'll see the on-ramp."

Andrew sits up. He opens the glove compartment and finds a pen. He motions to me that he wants paper.

I thank the couple and wish them a long and happy life.

Andrew writes on his hand. "Turn left," I read.

I go to the high school and turn left. There are houses across the road from the school. Andrew takes my left hand off the steering wheel and writes a number on my palm. I drive until I find the house. It has a high wall around it. I stop, but keep the engine running. "What are we doing?" I ask.

Andrew writes on his hand. I hold it in mine to see. "Mandela bitch," I read. Andrew jabs a finger at the house before reaching into his pocket and holding the tongue out to me. I take it and open the door. It lies raspy and dry in my hand, like the body of a bottom dweller exposed to the doom of fresh air and sunshine. When I look up Andrew is miming what I have to do.

Andrew gets out on the other side and pulls himself along to the base of the wall. He writes on his hand. *Sangoma curse you shout.* He reaches for my hand. When my palm is filled with words, I find the lid of a shoe box blown into a shrub hugging the wall, and he continues writing on that. He mimes instructions.

I pull myself up the wall and sit on top with a leg hanging down each side. I put the tongue on the brick surface between my legs where I can see it. I read out the curse. No, I do not read. I declaim: *Those whose voices you have taken curse you. They curse you with the gift of speech. You will speak, and speak, and not be able to stop. Your words will condemn you. Your husband will turn against you, and your children will deny you. You will wish for the power of silence, but it will not come to you.* I hold the tongue for a moment, then toss it onto the roof like a discus. After leaving my hand it is suddenly graceful, transformed by flight like the reptilian creatures who first conceived of diving into nothingness.

Ten minutes later we are at Baragwanath having Uncle Broer's cut sutured. The doctor puts her hand under his chin and lifts his head. "Pakamisa," she says. "Like so."

"Pezulu," Uncle Broer says. He strokes the doctor's arm. "Doc-terr." He strokes the shoulder of the Taiwanese nurse who is assisting. "*Chimerazania.*" He laughs.

Behind us Andrew is doing wheelies in a wheelchair he has found. He sneaks up to the nurse, and picks a notebook from her pocket. He writes something and shows it to her. She covers her mouth with her hand and looks the other way.

Andrew backs away, and I follow him. "What the hell happened out there?" I ask. "Why did everyone start beating up on everyone else?"

Andrew writes. "You were going to leave me there," I read.

"I thought you would be okay," I say.

"Because I'm black?" Andrew writes. "You know what Xoliswe Falati said while he was cutting me? 'Why you so black?' he said. 'You as black as fuckin coal. If I had petrol I'd burn you.'" He leaves me with the pad in my hand.

After a while he is back. He takes the pad and writes some more. "What did you say?"

I tell him about my natural history lesson.

Chimer-AZANIA? he asks.

I say yes.

He snorts and hisses. It is definitely a laugh. The nurse looks toward him, and he smiles at her. In between the laughs and smiles he writes. Gradually the entire alphabet of politics appears on the sheet. ANC UDF PAC AZAPO BC. When he is done, I understand that after Steve Biko was killed by police, a splinter group of his disciples under the leadership of Bishop Tutu joined forces with Mandela's ANC. The purists, to whom Halftime belongs, are still clinging to the ideas of Black Consciousness. The altercation from which we have fled was typical: the followers of the two greatest black leaders of the century, Mandela and Biko, are killing each other at the slightest provocation. Azania was *Biko's* name for the new South Africa. "When you say *Azania*, you pick a leader," Andrew explains.

When we drive home, Uncle Broer is asleep on the backseat. I am alone up front. Andrew has decided not to come home with us. The nurse thought she might be able to put him up for the night, he said. "Maybe she can get me a job in Taiwan," was the last thing Andrew wrote. Who knows. Maybe.

I find my way to the highway on-ramp. Under the glow of the crime lights Uncle Broer looks deathly pale, but so do my hands on the steering wheel. I reach back and feel his hand. It is warm and limp around the box of Disney character band-aids the nurse has given him.

I want to go home to Christine, but I need some time to think. I take the Bez Valley turnoff and drive to my quarry. Where the road ends, I park and walk the last half a kilometer over the greenish-grey lava that sealed up the basin soon after the gold was laid down. Somewhere beneath my feet is the Carbon Leader.

The loose mosaic of shale crunches under my shoes. I pick up a handful of shards and one by one I skip them off the worked face, where, if you look closely, you can see the fossil ripples left on the sand of the shore 2.4 billion years ago. *Much later, when geological time had fallen into history, the people of ancient Colchis placed sheepskins on the beds of streams to catch alluvial gold, thus giving rise to the legend of the golden fleece.* I sit down, my back against the face. Above the horizon, where daylight is bleeding up over the ridge, Orion is lying on his side. No one who sees him only before he sets will believe how he strides the night on his hands with his legs kicked deep into space. I watch him until the day erases him.

I must have dozed. The grind of shoes on gravel wakes me. I don't open my eyes. I recognize Uncle Broer's slow shuffle punctuated, I imagine, by stoops to pick up rocks. When he reaches me, he sits down too close like a kid. I can feel his breath on my face.

"Doc-torr?"

I look, and he's as close as my shaving face in the mirror.

He has rocks for me, handfuls. I take one and tap it sharply against a projection on the quarry face. It easily splits along the bedding plane. I show him how the two parts fit together, like a mold and cast. I point out the features of the parting, the wrinkles in the clay, the cracks formed by drying. "No bugs," I say.

Uncle Broer takes that as a challenge. He takes his own rocks one by one and strikes them against the face. He has a system. He takes from the right pocket, taps, and transfers to the left pocket. When he is through, he reverses the process. It is sort of peaceful. Like knowing what is going to happen from minute to minute.

My eyes are closed. The rhythm of Uncle Broer's blows lulls me like a lullaby. I dream vividly about an ostrich I had as a child. I am going to ride it, and my father is holding the sack over its head so I can mount. In my dream I know I'll never get on, because my father is dead. I wake, feeling relieved.

The sound has stopped. Uncle Broer is holding something out to me. "Metathorax," he says.

I blink, then focus. From Uncle Broer's rock an almost intact specimen of a large trilobite species stares out at the world for the first time in 300 million years. It bulges from the bedding plane like a wood carving, a wood louse grown to the size of a mouse. They are a dime a dozen, as the Americans would say, in this bed. Roaches of the Paleozoic. Adapted to every niche. Nevertheless, this is a very nice specimen. I give it back to Uncle Broer. "Actually," I say, "in a tri-lo-bite the tail end is not called a metathorax. It's called the py-gi-dium."

"Py-gi-dium," Uncle Broer says. "Pig police. Right on."

I stand in the bedroom door and watch Christine sleep. The lights are off, but morning glimmers blue through the window. There are indications that she is faking. One, she is on her own side of the bed. Usually, when she has the bed to herself, she sprawls diagonally into my space. Two, the radio is on. Christine cannot sleep with the radio on.

I hold my breath and listen. Today, October ninth, the announcer says, marks the would-be fiftieth birthday of John Lennon, who, ten years ago, celebrated his fortieth birthday with the release of what would be his last album.

What kind of a sentence is that?

I sit on the edge of the bed. I stick my hand into the covers and find Christine's knee. "My new species," I say. "I'm going to name it after you. After us both. *Lawsonia Odendalia.*"

"They've named four asteroids for the Beatles," she says. "Number four thousand forty-seven is Lennon." She pulls a pillow over her head and starts crying. The bed shivers with her gasps for air.

I lie down beside her and wedge my head in under the pillow next to hers. A few breaths later her trembling intakes of air come to a stop. She turns on her side with her back toward me. We fit together, part and counterpart. *Splitting a rock at the bedding plane cannot yield a clear division with the entire organism (the part) on one surface, and only the impression (the counterpart) on the other. Any split must leave some pieces of the organism on one side, other bits on the opposite block.* With an ear to the mattress I can hear the beat of my heart reverberating in the spaces among the springs that keep our spines straight.

I reach a hand under her nightshirt and mold my hand to the soft comfort of her breast. She layers her hand over mine and presses it tighter against her skin.

"I mean it," I say. "I'm going to marry you. And go with you. I want to. *Whither thou goest I will go.*"

I don't know if she is hearing me. I think of the American Charles Doolittle Walcott, who packed up the entire cache of fossils from Canada's Burgess Shale and carted it back to America. Christine strokes my hand a few times, then pushes aside the pillow to open a space for her mouth. "It's twenty years already," she says, "since they killed John Lennon. She's been a widow twenty years."

"He has a kid," I say.

"Raising a kid by oneself," she says.

"The kid's all right," I say. "He used to build jigsaw puzzles with the picture-side down. By the shape alone. I used to do that. When I was a kid."

She shudders in breath.

"My new creature," I say. "He looks like the coat of arms on the Isle of Man."

"*Whither thou goest I will go* was said by a woman to a woman," she says.

I nuzzle my face into the hollow between her shoulder and head. Her carotid pulses against my lips. "Lennon in the sky with diamonds," I say.

"Galaxies get numbers only," Christine says. "And craters on planets can only be named for dead people. That is the rule."

I think of my father snug in his pocket of earth, his hair thick with gold from a percolating stream. I put my hand behind her head and turn her face toward me. She does not resist. I breathe her breath.

ACKNOWLEDGMENTS

I gratefully recognize my mother, Susan Steenekamp, and my mother-in-law, Raaitjie Saunders, as the tellers of the many stories-within-stories that appear in this collection. I would like to thank Kirstin Scott, Jan Stucki, Brandon Griggs, Ann Kelly, Lynne Butler Oaks, and Shen Christenson for the feedback, the friendship, and the food. I am grateful to Kirstin Scott and her father, Bill Scott, for agreeing to grace the cover, and to Sean Graff for permission to use the cover photo. I am thankful to Kathryn Lang at SMU Press for her sharp editorial insight and continuous support.

I gratefully acknowledge the support of the Utah Arts Council, which awarded this collection the 1997 prize for a book-length work of short fiction (judged by Enid Shomer, New York) and the 1998 publication prize for a book-length work (judged by Rick Campbell of Anhinga Press, Florida).

I further gratefully acknowledge the following works, which appear in or inform the stories:

The collection title, *Blessings on the Sheep Dog*, is taken from a description in *National Geographic*, August 1978, of a plaque commemorating the contribution of collies to the sheep farming economy in New Zealand. "My Brother Can Tell" is in part inspired by an article in *Omni*, July 1982, about the music in our genes. I am grateful to Keith Davis for helping prepare the musical notation appearing in "My Brother Can Tell" and for his permission to include it here. I quote from Shabbir Banoobhai's poem "the border" in "My Brother Can Tell"; "the border" originally appeared in *echoes of my other self*, Ravan Press, South Africa, 1980, and is reproduced here with the poet's permission. The passage about Beethoven's *Eroica* in "My Brother Can Tell" is adapted from pp. 150–152 of *The Music Man*, by Yehudi Menuhin and Curtis W. Davis, published by Macdonald General Books, London and Sydney, 1979. References to the songs of the humpback whales on the Voyager spacecraft in "We'll Get to Now Later" are indebted to *Cosmos*, by Carl Sagan, published by Macdonald, London, 1981; the italicized lines at the end of the story are adapted from the same source.

I acknowledge the help of Joe Wysong of the Gestalt Journal Press to establish that the original source of the old woman/young woman picture in "The Epistemology of Romantic Despair" is the British humor magazine *Punch*, 1915, and that the picture is now in the public domain. The illustration from Aristotle's *De Caelo* is reproduced in "The Epistemology of Romantic Despair" as published in S.K. Heninger, Jr., *Touches of Sweet Harmony: Pythagorean Cosmology and Renaissance Poetics*, p. 123, San Marino, California, 1974. This illustration is used by permission of the Huntington Library. The passage about the circle of fifths is adapted from *The Music Man*, cited previously, pp. 28–29. I would like to thank Michael Lindsay for creating the graphical representation of the circle of fifths in "The Epistemology of Romantic Despair" and for his permission to include it here; thanks also to Shelley Turley for the sketch of Shrödinger's cat in the same story and for her permission to print it. I acknowledge the help of the Penguin Press, London, in helping to establish the source of the Jabberwocky reversed script that is reproduced in "The Epistemology of Romantic Despair"; their permissions editor traced it to Lewis Carroll's original edition of *Through the Looking-Glass* (illustrated by John Tenniel), material that is now in the public domain. The Jabberwocky script and explanation appear in the story as published in Martin Gardner's *The Annotated Alice: Alice's Adventures in Wonderland* and *Through the Looking-Glass by Lewis Carroll with an Introduction and Notes*, Penguin Books, Chaucer Press, Suffolk, England, 1960.

The chaos theory in "No Money for Stamps" is informed by Ilya Prigogine and Isabelle Stengers's *Order out of Chaos: Man's New Dialogue with Nature*, Bantam Books, New York, 1984. The paleontology in "Walking Legs" is in part informed by Stephen Jay Gould's *Wonderful Life: The Burgess Shale and the Nature of History*, W.W. Norton & Co., New York, N.Y., 1989; the italicized lines on pp. 194, 224, and 239 and the descriptions of the arthropods on pp. 230–231 are adapted from the same source. The paleontology in "Walking Legs" is in part informed also by A.R. Willcox's *Southern Land: The Prehistory of Southern Africa*,

Purnell and Sons (SA) Pty Ltd, Cape Town, 1976; the italicized lines on p. 237 have been adapted from the same source.

Some of the stories in this collection appeared first in the following publications: "We'll Get to Now Later," *Western Humanities Review* vol. 49 (3), 196–211, 1995 (University of Utah), first place in the 1995 fiction contest, judged by Stephen Dixon; "My Brother Can Tell," *Nebraska Review* vol. 42 (2), 7–19, 1996 (University of Nebraska, Omaha), first place in the 1996 fiction contest, judged by James Reed; "Blessings on the Sheep Dog," *New Letters* vol. 63 (2), 57–70, 1997 (University of Missouri, Kansas City), second runner-up, 1996 fiction contest, judged by Larry Woiwode; "The Epistemology of Romantic Despair," *Western Humanities Review* Fiftieth Anniversary Issue vol. 50 (4), 298–309, 1996 (White Heath, Illinois), third place winner, 1996 fiction contest; "Walking Legs," *Quarterly West* vol. 45, 14–40, 1997 (University of Utah, Salt Lake City), winner of the 1997 novella contest.

Photograph by Sean Graff

In 1984 GERDA SAUNDERS emigrated to the United States from South Africa, where she had worked as a research scientist and math and physics teacher. Upon her arrival in this country, she began writing fiction. She became a U.S. citizen in 1992, and in 1996 she received a Ph.D. in English from the University of Utah. She now designs multi-media instructional materials for computer- and Web-based training. She and her husband Peter make their home in Salt Lake City. They have two children who attend the University of Utah. She recently completed her first novel, *The Last Pietà of MichelAgniolo*.